Z1
20.11

THE WALK TO
ACORN BRIDGE

THE WALK TO
ACORN BRIDGE

John Treherne

JONATHAN CAPE
THIRTY-TWO BEDFORD SQUARE LONDON

First published 1989
© John Treherne 1989
Jonathan Cape Ltd,
32 Bedford Square, London WC1B 3SG

A CIP catalogue record for this book
is available from the British Library

ISBN 0–224–02629–1

Printed and bound in Great Britain by
Butler & Tanner Ltd, Frome and London

To my Father

PART ONE

Chick-Chack Day
1900

ONE

It is the first thing I can remember clearly, the trek to Acorn Bridge to see the railway engine. It was probably Tiger's idea. We were climbing the steep thistle-dotted slope of the coombe and as we came level with the tops of the farmyard elms we glimpsed far across the Vale a white streak moving steadily across the flat landscape like a skein of wool on a patchwork quilt. We had spotted it many times before, ever since our legs could carry us past the watercress beds and up on the chalk track to the first rising slope of the downs. But we had never seen the mysterious machine that smudged the horizon. In fact, we had seen hardly anything. None of us had ever crossed the parish boundary.

I suppose it was the excitement of Chick-Chack Day that put the idea in our heads. On that day – the 29th of May – the village boys wore fresh sprigs of oak and ash in their button-holes or pinned to their caps. We had no idea why. But it made us feel important and we chanted after anyone caught without their emblems

> Chick-Chack
> Powder monkey!
> You're the biggest fool
> Around the country!

We had been bundled out of the house, as we were every morning – including Sundays – summer or winter. My father was second ploughman and on summer mornings he got up at half-past four to feed his team. My mother laboured wherever she could, scrubbing the broad brick floor of the farm kitchen or out on the fields picking up flints for the roads, pulling docks or, at harvest time, gleaning the stubble. When she left our cottage, the rickety green door slammed shut with a jingling clatter.

Ruth, my elder sister must have been about ten on the day we walked to the railway; she had charge of the 'little'un', my younger sister. She must have been passing four years old. She was a mischievous child when she had anything like enough to eat.

I did not see where they went that morning, but it must have been to the rickyard. Ruth had hollowed out a sort of nest for them at the bottom of one of the stacks, from which they would make forays to the brook to drink from folded dock leaves, or hang around the door of the farmhouse kitchen when bacon was boiling, or fling sticks at rickyard cats.

Ruth never came with us and we would have punched her if she had tried. Yet when we came down from the coombe she was watching us through the cowyard gate, the little'un at her side. She did not speak – she rarely did – but she had guessed that something was up. I suppose our excitement was so patent. We were such grand fellows that morning, Chick-Chack greenery at our breasts, running down on the springy turf, kicking at the young thistles and shouting with the excitement of it all. There had been nothing like it before, this march to Acorn Bridge to see the engine. The sight of my two sisters gazing solemnly through the cowyard gate added spice to the adventure. We slowed down, the better for them to appreciate our importance, the four of us marching in line.

I can see it now, that May morning in 1900, with our shadows falling long and thin before us on the grass. Tiger was in front, swinging along in huge baggy shorts cut down from his father's breeches but still falling well below his knees, then me and Jess, his shorn red hair sticking up like chestnut spines, and at the rear Pebbie, fat and perspiring, an enormous straw hat supported on his ears to hide his scalp, which was crusted with impetigo. We turned back along the farm lane and then round by the watercress beds, to the lazy murmuring of coots. Once we were out of sight of Ruth and the little'un, we did not have to hide our excitement. Jess began chanting, 'Chick-Chack powder monkey . . . ' but he stopped when he realised how inadequate it sounded. Ours was a manly enterprise and 'Chick-Chack' would not do. Then Tiger turned, his dark gipsy eyes glittering.

'Bugger,' he shouted.

'Bugger, bugger – bugger, the bugger.'

This exhilarating masculine word was the forbidden currency of Jem the fogger and of Sammy Hill who got drunk: rough, violent men of uncertain temper. It was never heard on female lips. We could not get enough of it.

'Bugger, bugger – bugger the bugger,' we responded while Tiger waved his arms as though conducting a choir. He paused, clearly feeling a need for something more inspiring.

'Bugger, bugger – the old cow's arse,' he roared.

'Bugger, bugger – the old cow's arse,' we bawled back.

Coot and moorhen alike scattered in alarm as we shouted and clattered between the beds of cress and tall, shading elms. We startled Granny Bowles as we passed her cottage. She waved her stick over the hedge and shook her head at our depravity. When we passed Jess's sister in the lane she threw her apron over her face and ran off giggling into the orchard. This was very satisfying.

By now we were level with the first of the two brick and chalk cob pillars that marked the entrance to the mill yard.

We were still shouting the few coarse words we could think of when the bailiff came out; he hit Tiger on the head with a huge fist, knocking him to the ground. He kicked at the rest of us as we scattered.

'You dirty young buggers,' he roared. 'I'll get you! Buggered if I don't.'

But we were off, racing away over the mill bridge.

We stopped, on the roadside beyond the last cottage. Tiger slumped down among the cow parsley, his dark head bent, and blubbered quietly. We stood looking down at him in a detached way, as children do when watching kittens being drowned or a cockerel having its neck wrung. I remember worrying that Tiger might give up, and that we would not get to the railway that day. None of us spoke. We just waited. Then Tiger looked up, his sallow face dirty and streaked with tears.

'Bugger, bugger – the old cow's arse,' he mumbled.

We answered him in subdued tones, but did not move until Tiger pushed himself to his feet.

'Come on,' he croaked.

We moved off steadfastly enough, in a very different temper now. It was not only that Tiger had been humiliated; we had begun to realise the magnitude of the adventure.

The road stretched flinty and straight from the downland skirts to an empty horizon wobbling in the early summer haze. On either side were wide grass verges and hedges that towered above us. The still valley air was already tinged with the smell of May blossom and the muskiness of cow parsley. There was an incessant hum of insects and the calling of yellowhammers. The flints reflected the heat back at us and pressed uncomfortably through the soles of our worn boots, so we waded, knee-deep in buttercups, along the grass of the roadside.

'How big will her be then, Tiger?'

For Jess, this was almost garrulous. We were a taciturn lot; we did not need to speak when nods and grunts would do. But Jess knew what he was doing, and so did we. His remark was formal acknowledgment of Tiger's leadership and allowed him to act as if he had not just been humiliated; it also marked the end of the high spirits which had us shouting and running through the watercress beds.

Tiger screwed up his face, considering.

'Big?'

'How big?' Jess persisted. 'How tall will her funnel be?'

There was no reply. Tiger bided his time and tried to look sagacious. The fact was, he had no idea what to say, for none of us had even seen a picture of a railway engine. There was a colour print on our cottage wall showing the Duke of Wellington at Waterloo, and there was an empty biscuit tin with the picture of a stage coach called 'On the Open Road' – as I learned later when I could read. There were no books. The family Bible was in Gran's cottage.

'Will her be as tall as the ploughing engine?' Jess ventured.

'Bigger,' Tiger decreed. 'Taller nor a haystack.'

There was silence as we digested this prediction. We were not surprised. We knew that these were exciting times. It was a constant theme of our parents' conversations – the passing of the good old days – and we could see for ourselves, every day, great churns – shining things of steel and brass – brim full of milk that were taken off and loaded on the railway to be in London that very day, so the carter boasted. Then there was the steam plough that had thundered away for a few glorious days in the autumn; and the soldiers who had ridden through the village and hauled their guns up the chalk track on to the downs to be followed by muffled thuddings which we had heard for the rest of the day.

Tiger plodded on in silence, buttercup pollen dusting his boots. We had walked prodigiously, further than we had ever been before. But the road still stretched away before us and if we looked back, the sunlit downs seemed as close as when we began.

There was no one in sight, only the four of us, traipsing along between the high walls of the blossomed hedges which seemed to enclose the heat. I was hungry and thirsty. It was so strange to us, this long flint road, for we had never before ventured so far into the valley.

Pebbie was feeling the heat and his head was itching. We sat down on the roadside to wait for him to cool off and scratch his scabs. It was then that Tiger spotted two small figures coming towards us from the direction of the village. Their silhouettes were unmistakable: Ruth and the little'un were following us. Tiger stood up and shook his fist. The two figures stopped – they were hand-in-hand – paused at the side of the road and then disappeared into the hedge.

Tiger decided to ignore them, hauled Pebbie to his feet, though he was still scratching and led the way northwards. There was no sign of my sisters, but we trotted on as quickly as we could, to shake them off in case they should try to follow. The going was easier now, for the flints had given way to a smoother dirt and gravel road. Without knowing it, we had crossed, for the first time, the frontier of Ashbourne parish. I began to sense differences that were oddly disturbing – not only underfoot and in the hedgerows, which were now taller than ever, but in the darker green of the leaves and the scraggier feel of the wayside flowers. The cattle smells lingered here, when they would have been blown away on the open downs; so would the swarms of voracious flies which hovered above our heads in black quivering clouds. There were peculiar things under the hedges, a huge fungus like a distorted ear and strange looking plants with fleshy leaves.

Our progress soon flagged. We seemed to be getting nowhere: the road stretched away into the heat haze; the downs still dominated the skyline behind us. But we dragged on until, quite spontaneously, we all tumbled down together into a clump of cow parsley to escape the insect swarms that were pursuing us.

Pebbie said that we should wait there to jump out at my sisters if they appeared.

We were hidden in lacy greenness, each huddled in his own leafy refuge, mating soldier beetles clinging to the grass halms around our faces. Tiger was making squeaking noises with a blade of grass pressed between his palms; Pebbie was silent, but I knew he was there all right – he smelled terribly, especially in hot weather. Jess was muttering about headless horsemen. He was fascinated by such things; they were the stock-in-trade of the stories which our parents regaled us with to frighten us into obedience with threats of how we would end up on the gallows if we did not mend our ways. Looking back, I realise that such epics as Wat Sannell's ride to Highworth were fragments of ancient lore, still half-believed in these times of steam power, milk churns and great traction engines. Their effect was to excite rather than frighten us, though spasms of fear could overtake us on autumn nights or even in broad daylight. Crouched among the cow parsley, poking at the soldier beetles with a bent of grass, I knew what Jess was worrying about: that this long straight road between the tall hedges was the way the headless horsemen came.

We were silent beneath the almost deafening insect hum, each of us apprehensive or cast down in this strange place.

Suddenly there was a clattering of wood pigeons followed by a crash in the hedge behind us. We all jumped up, lashing at the waiting flies which immediately resumed their battering against our faces. Then, Jess let out a yelp, staring pop-eyed at the opposite hedgerow – from which my sister's face was gazing with the same doleful expression as when she had watched us from the cowyard gate.

'You daft old cow!' Jess shrieked and rushed at Ruth with both fists clenched.

Ruth stepped on to the road, knocked him down with a single blow in the stomach and then turned to face Tiger. It was a tense moment, for I knew only too well the strain of reckless madness that was in Tiger. He was not a strong fighter. I could knock him over or wrestle him down and sit on his chest, glaring into his dark, gipsy face. But Tiger would never give up. However many times he was brought down he would come up again and fling himself at me. It was not so much this rage which made him so formidable: it was the sheer boredom of repeatedly knocking him over that made him indestructible and our acknowledged leader. It was how he got his name, from one of the labourers who had watched us scrapping in the rickyard when we were small. There was something sinister about Tiger.

By this time, the little'un had emerged from a gap in

16

the hedge and was standing next to Ruth, looking down nervously at Jess, who was rolling on the grass, clutching his abdomen. Tiger just stood staring at the girls, hitching up his breeches, the bottoms of which were now half-way down his calves. He did not seem to be going to do anything, so I stepped forward to give Ruth a good thump, for I felt a certain family responsibility for this latest turn of events.

Ruth jabbed me in the belly: it hurt like anything and I doubled up, my eyes watering. I was totally surprised, because my sister was usually so docile; she had never done anything like this before. Even in my agony — trying desperately not to cry — I remember hearing Tiger laugh and then Pebbie join in with a snigger.

I managed to stand up, still half-blinded with tears, and aimed a kick at Pebbie. Pebbie avoided my boot but lost his straw hat and exposed his oozing scalp to the insects. He clapped his hat back on his head and, in so doing, trapped a crowd of buzzing flies beneath it.

He was now hopping around in the middle of the road, alternately removing and replacing his hat.

He would probably have remained in this predicament, had it not been for the little'un who brandished a leafy elder branch, which, I had not noticed, she was dragging behind her. With a strenuous effort, she lifted the branch above her head. I thought she was going to whack Pebbie with it and was pleased that she at least was on my side, especially as I had pinched her leg rather badly that morning. But no, she was trying to hold the thing over Pebbie's head. Pebbie grabbed it from her and waggled it over his scalp with a look of blissful gratitude before replacing his hat.

By this time, Tiger had lost patience and was walking purposefully away as though glad to be rid of us. We did not follow immediately but dived into the hedge to wrench off branches to keep away the flies – like Ruth and the little'un.

I tried one last throw against Ruth.

'You get off back,' I said. 'We don't want you.' But she took no notice and I did not fancy trying to thump her again, so I let the matter drop and plodded after Jess and Pebbie.

Tiger kept up a brisk pace, with Jess, Pebbie and me in line behind, bearing our elder branches triumphantly aloft like fluttering banners. None of us spoke; we just kept going, clumping along, our clumsy hand-me-down boots kicking up the dust behind us. On and on we traipsed, with never a backward glance.

The ordeal was not so much the fatigue of the journey as the enforced monotony of our effort – the endless putting of one foot in front of the other. We were like puppies on a treadmill and it was all of our own making, this desire to see the railway engine. Not that this was foremost in our minds as we plodded along between tall hedges on our journey. Now all we wanted was to reach the end of that never-ending road.

It seemed an age before I looked back. The sun-dappled downs now looked further away, and there in the middle of the road, some hundred yards back, was Ruth with the little'un – pick-a-back – holding the elder branch over them both. I plodded on with murder in my heart and a gnawing in my belly.

We were always hungry in those days. But things had been more than usually difficult that morning, with trouble at home about the pigs' barley. There was a bit of land that came with our cottage; it was steep and difficult to plough and the farmer let it go with the cottage. Father grew cabbages and some potatoes – monstrous great things we used to call 'earth-heavers' – a few summer vegetables and a patch of barley that he mowed by hand. He sent the barley to the mill to be ground into meal and for the rest of the year fed it, with whatever else he could find, to our pigs. Father sold the animals to buy clothes and pots and pans and pay the rent, which was near impossible on thirteen shillings a week.

There was no spare cash for anything but the barest of essentials. Yet Mother would still prepare occasional treats for us. She would bake a lardy cake in the farm kitchen, if she could get permission, or make us lolli-pops from lumps of lard dipped in sugar. As it was Chick-Chack Day, she had tried that morning to make us barley bangers. This she did by sifting the pigs' meal, mixing it with water and baking it in a pot on the fire. On that day, Father had caught her at it and there was the devil of a row.

'You'd starve my pigs to feed they blasted young 'uns,' he shouted as we made our escape. Father was a hard man − he had to be − and often violent, especially when he came back from the alehouse, but he never spared himself. If he was given a lump of spoiled cheese or a piece of bacon at the farm, he never ate it but saved it to give to us when he came back in the evening, as often as not gnawing away at a slice of swede taken from the farmyard clamp.

We were expert scavengers − sucking nectar from cowslip flowers, rubbing ripening ears of wheat and barley between our grubby palms to separate the grains, plucking sorrel leaves, pulling swedes, scrumping apples, picking blackberries and gathering hazel nuts, but early summer was a lean time and there were only hawthorn leaves; 'bread and cheese' we used to call the buds and young leaves. I stopped to pick some from among the cascades of white blossom. The others joined in, including Tiger, who turned back, and Ruth and the little'un, who had caught up.

Tiger squared up to Ruth: he had got bored with 'bread and cheese' which was by now already dark green and very chewy.

'What you following us for?'

Ruth continued plucking at the hawthorn. Tiger repeated his question; Ruth turned to face him.

'Where you goin', then?' she said.

Tiger ignored this

'Why're you following us for?'

'I got to − got to keep an eye on him,' Ruth replied jerking her head in my direction. 'Ma will wallop me if I don't.'

'Well, you can't come with us. Not unless . . . ' Tiger faltered searching for inspiration, his dark eyes glittering. 'Not unless . . . you pull down your drawers.'

Ruth paused to consider this, pushing her dark hair from her face.

'Not in front of them I don't.' Ruth again looked in my direction, a half smile on her face.

Tiger considered the matter, trying to look important, hitching up his sagging breeches and swiping at the insects.

'You can do it behind the hedge then,' Tiger said with an imperious sweep of his arm.

'Not 'til you tell me where we're going,' Ruth retorted.

'To see the railway engine . . . ' Jess piped up as Tiger landed out at him and glared at Ruth who was now looking thoughtful.

'How do you know this is the way?' she laughed.

No one replied: her question was too awful to contemplate. The fact was that we had no idea where that road led. We had just followed Tiger. After all, from the village, it had seemed to point in the direction from where, on the downs, we had seen the railway smoke.

'Well?' Ruth persisted. 'How?'

'Corse it goes to the railway engine,' Tiger blustered.

'How do you know it do? How do you know it do go *anywhere*?' Ruth continued remorselessly. 'How do you know it don't stop? How do you know it don't *turn* and go somewhere else? How do you know?'

I was overwhelmed. I had never heard my sister speak more than two words together before. So was Pebbie. He had suffered more than any of us from the rigours of the march and was near breaking-point.

'Yes. How do we know?' he burst out, his fat face streaked with sweat, his straw hat jiggling on his head with agitation. 'The waggon don't go this way.'

Pebbie was right: the brimming churns that were loaded in the dairy yard each morning were hauled to the railway along the big road that ran westward, parallel with the escarpment of the downs.

'This is the way, I tell you,' shouted Tiger, his dark cheeks flushed with anger, as he flung himself at Pebbie. The two of them wrestled on the ground, Pebbie on top, until Tiger bit him on the neck and then crouched over him, kneeing him in the back.

We stood watching and then backed away as Tiger rose to his feet, giving Pebbie a final kick. A good inch of striped shirt protruded through a tear in his trousers. Pebbie remained where he lay, roaring with fright. Tiger stepped towards Ruth, thought better of whatever he was going to do and then strode to the hedgerow and tore free an elderberry branch. Without another word, he turned northward along the road.

It was some time before the rest of us moved. Jess was the first to do so, raising his leafy standard and starting off after Tiger. Then, to my surprise, Ruth followed – hauling the little'un who was sobbing loudly – holding her branch high. There seemed nothing for it but for me to follow, leaving Pebbie still lying in the road.

TWO

Like much else in our downland village in those days our
childish friendships were threadbare affairs: shifting and
often violent alliances between potential belligerents.
Perhaps they always are unless softened by the luxury of
better times; ours were stripped to the bone by hardship
and deprivation.

That is why I could leave Pebbie – fat and smelly and
hungry, with his head covered in scabs – weeping in the
dirt of a country lane, to follow someone who had
talked dirty to the sisters whose existence I only
acknowledged with spiteful punches and who hardly
cared two acorns for me.

I did not look back after the fight in the road on
Chick-Chack Day, I merely left Pebbie and followed
Tiger and Jess and my sisters on our journey.

I had plenty to worry about as I trudged behind Jess.
Why had Ruth followed us? I certainly did not believe
the story she told Tiger about having to keep her eye on
me. How could she have done? Every other day we
were crow starving or up on the downs or messing
about by the watercress beds – and she never followed
us to these places. Then there was that daftness of
Tiger's about taking down her drawers. And why was

she still dragging the little'un all this way after going on about it not being the right way?

We did not get far on the next stage of the journey. Tiger's feet were troubling him and he squatted down at the roadside, grumbling under his breath and looking daggers at the little'un.

Our boots were handed down from child to child. Tiger had acquired his prematurely, and they slithered like barges on his bare feet: his skinny ankles were rubbed raw.

Old and worn though they were, our boots were treasured possessions. Mine were a good pair. They had cost several shillings and were made in the village by Jimmie Bunce – so Father used to boast – but he must have died before I was born for I certainly cannot remember him. There was, in fact, no shoe-maker in Ashbourne when I was a boy and our rough footwear was mended by old Launcelot Horton who had been a shepherd, but had set himself up as a cobbler after he developed a limp and could no longer manage the long walks over the downs.

We used to boast to one another about our boots – even when they were falling to pieces – emphasising their superiority with kicks. So Tiger must have been doubly-resentful as he sat by the roadside nursing his feet.

It was Ruth who helped Tiger, kneeling before him, her long black skirt sweeping the dirt. She tore up handfuls of grass, picked dock leaves and pushed them into the empty spaces around Tiger's ankles.

Pebbie rolled up as we were watching Ruth and stood behind her, a trickle of blood still oozing from the weal on his neck where Tiger had bitten him.

Standing there, tired and very thirsty, I felt again – only now more strongly – the strangeness of the place.

We had been walking for what seemed like hours along that leafy corridor with hardly a gate to break the monotony, and they only revealed enclosed fields of lush meadow grass. It was as though we were walking through an empty land. Occasionally there were faint boomings mingled with the insect hum, like the guns we had heard on the downs or like distant thunder, although there was now not a cloud in sight. A cuckoo called, close at hand; a large white bird glided over our heads – a barn owl in broad daylight – and flapped silently along the hedgerow.

Then we saw the waggon in the middle of the road. Quite close it was, coming towards us, drawn by two black shire-horses. A familiar enough sight for country children, but its abrupt appearance took us unawares – we had not noticed that the road ahead was curving – and there was no driver, just the empty waggon and the great horses moving steadily along. Without a word we stood and watched it pass, saw the long whip sticking up where the driver should have been and a gaitered leg lying across the seat.

We knew that waggon, we saw it every day *and* its sleeping driver, but in that green secret place it was strange and disturbing.

Tiger grunted, picked up his elder branch and walked on, his ankles fringed in greenery. No one spoke. We just plodded on, following the curving road. My feet were aching, my throat parched – from thirst and a kind of fear.

The hedgerow was thinning now; there were two hayricks standing at the edge of a field. Jess spotted a black cat watching us from a clump of cow parsley and flung a stick at it.

Then Tiger began talking of the engine that we would see. It could not be long now, he said, perhaps round the next bend. There was no answer, for we knew he was trying to convince himself that the road led to where he hoped.

'It'll have a chimney all right,' Tiger said.

'It'll be like a gurt cannon on a wooden carriage,' Pebbie chimed in. He had evidently recovered from his beating and was trying to curry favour with Tiger.

We all nodded. It was an exciting, if improbable, prospect.

'And we'll be able to get some water,' Tiger continued. 'There'll be some – they'll need it for the engine.'

'God almighty,' Jess replied – it was one of his father's expressions. 'God almighty, I could do with a mouthful of water.'

The black cat had now reappeared and was sitting in the road ahead. Jess searched for another missile, but the animal shot beneath a small gate in a low privet hedge on our right from which we glimpsed a slate roof and then dull red brickwork. It was like a child's drawing of a house, with a white wooden porch, green front door and sash windows – two up and two down. Everything in the garden was neat and tidy; bursting with flowers, alive with bees, with rows of flowering broad-bean plants in which the cat had taken shelter. A blackbird was chittering away in alarm on the brick path.

'Go on then,' Jess whispered to me. 'Go and ask for some water.'

Out of bravado, and because Tiger was hanging back, I started off up the path leaving the others standing nervously at the gate. I could hear faint noises coming from the house, rhythmical ones it seemed and, as I drew closer, what sounded like wailing in a cracked and high-pitched voice.

It was really very frightening, but I could not resist

creeping up to the window on the left-hand side of the porch. It was gloomy at first, but as my eyes adapted to the shadows I saw an old lady pedalling away at an instrument on the other side of a room, which was stuffed with furniture and knick-knacks, her hands moving like lightning over the keys. I had never seen a room like that – let alone a harmonium – and at the time had no idea what she was singing except that it sounded like a hymn.

There was a mirror on the harmonium. She saw my reflection in it and was across the room and out through the front door before I could untangle myself from a rose bush and leg it down the path.

'You come here you young devil,' she squeaked, grabbing my arm. 'What on earth are you doing? And where do you come from anyway?'

'Ashbourne,' I replied in some agitation, for all old ladies were potential witches – especially if they had black cats and behaved like this one. 'We want some water, Missus.'

'We? What do ye mean "We"?' she shouted. 'I don't see no one else.'

'They're behind the hedge . . .'

'Well, they'd better come out – or I'll pull your arm off.'

One by one the heads appeared over the hedge.

'Please, Missus,' Tiger called. 'Could we have some water?'

The old lady regarded Tiger, shaking me absent-mindedly as she did so. Even as she jerked me back and forth, I noticed that she had exceptionally long nostrils, a lump on her neck and that she sort of quivered all the time.

'Water?' she screeched. 'It'll cost you a farthing. You'll have to pay me a farthing.'

26

'We ain't got no money, Missus,' Tiger called back.

'A farthing,' she continued. 'When I was a girl I used to swallow a worm for a farthing. Gurt big'uns. They didn't half wriggle. Used to get a farthing I did.'

'But we ain't got a farthing, Missus,' Tiger protested.

'Well, you'll have to swallow a worm then.'

'No, I won't,' said Tiger.

'Won't get no water then,' came the reply.

'Aw, come on, Missus,' Pebbie pleaded.

The crone glared at Pebbie, who had removed his hat to fan his damp face.

'What's the matter with his head?' she demanded, addressing her question to me.

'Scabs,' I said. 'He got scabs.'

'I can see that, you daft little devil,' she cackled, and stopped shaking me in her mirth. 'Badger's grease, that's what he wants. Cure anything like, that badger's grease will.'

She paused, as if to recall more nuggets of wisdom.

'Beat a badger to death once when I was a girl. Our Dad left it outside in a sack and I beat it to death with a stick. Damn gurt stick it were.'

'Coo, you didn't really, did you, Missus?' Jess gasped.

'I did – with a gurt stick.'

I renewed my struggling, but to no avail.

'Kip still will you boy,' she said shaking me in her bony little hands until my teeth rattled. 'You're all the same from Ashbourne. An okkard lot and always hungry. Hungry Ashbourne, we call it down here. Do they still give you pebble soup up there, boy?'

She gave another cackle, dragged me round the side of the house and pushed me through a door in a lean-to built on at the back.

I was overwhelmed by the splendour of that wooden kitchen: everything was gleaming, with a black-leaded range and, most marvellous, a shining brass pump. There was a smell of polish and baking. Above a sink was a lace-curtained window; on an oil-cloth covered table was a large lardy cake.

'Here, grab hold of that,' she ordered, still holding on to my arm which was numb from the tightness of her grip.

My grubby fingers were glued to the surface of the cake by its toffee stickiness. The crone propelled me back to my companions. She was holding something behind her back.

'Come you here,' she commanded.

Pebbie moved cautiously forward, his brown eyes round with wonder at the object I was carrying.

'Come on then, get hold of it!' she screeched, her old head wobbling with vexation.

Pebbie advanced slowly, his eyes fixed on the lardy cake. As he took it, the crone let go of my arm, grabbed Pebbie's ear and began vigorously dabbing away at the top of his head with a blue-bag. Pebbie howled with fright at the application of this household object, which was used to bleach the washing, but he hung on to the lardy cake and, when she released him, ran full tilt for the gate with me behind him.

We collected together in the road, Pebbie still muttering. His scalp was now pale blue.

'What about a mouthful of water to go with the lardy cake, Missus?' Tiger called out to the old woman, who was now standing at the gate.

'You'll have to get it from the ditch down there as you ain't got a farthing.'

With that, she disappeared. Shortly after, we could just make out the sound of the harmonium and a faint warbling of 'Lead Kindly Light'.

THREE

Pebbie carried the lardy cake high, his straw hat jammed down on to his ears. This was Pebbie's triumph, his glory: a moment such as he had never known in his life. We followed, our hunger sharpened by expectation. The little'un was chuckling, and Jess grinned like an idiot. Even the prospect of ditch water was not so daunting. After all, we tried some queer things in those days. Jess's family had even eaten snails, big Roman ones and his father was still known as Sluggie Bunce in the village. Mother was not above cooking charlock, stinging-nettles, sorrel or rhubarb leaves when the going was bad.

But above everything, we wanted cake: we craved for it, lusted after it. It was always lardy cake; sticky, sweet and satisfying, slipping like greasy cannon-balls into our empty stomachs. Like so many things in the faltering economy of our cottage, it depended on pigs, on great gobbets of lard that were smeared on warm dough, sprinkled with sugar and currants, folded over and over and then baked in a meat tin – if you had an oven. We had lard with everything in those days – spread on bread, dipped in sugar for sweetmeats or rubbed in to cure skin complaints – and our bacon, which we liked to eat raw, was mostly fat. The trouble was that father sold our pigs and we never got enough of anything – certainly not lardy cake.

Pebbie led the way to the ditch. We couldn't see it at first, but Pebbie shoved his way through the hedge at the northern boundary of the old lady's garden, and there it was – a clear little stream running beside a tree-lined meadow, disappearing through a culvert under the road.

'Not a bad old ditch, this,' said Tiger.

We fell on our knees, scooping and slurping away with our cupped hands like thirsty animals. It had a queer, earthy tang, quite different from the water of the chalk land, but it softened our parched lips and its coolness spread through our bodies.

The sun was now high in the sky. We retreated to the shade of an overhanging willow and waited anxiously while Pebbie fussed on about dividing up the lardy cake. In the end it was Ruth who broke it up carefully into five portions, with a small one for the little'un torn from her own. I noticed that Ruth was pretty, with her high colour and long dark hair. It must have been the first time that I did so: perhaps it had something to do with that jab in the stomach.

Ruth handed out the lumps of cake, one by one, starting with Pebbie. She did it with an earnest expression of hers, biting at her lower lip. We were all affected by the occasion. It was the first time that anything had been entirely ours, to divide and share as we chose. And it was such a glorious thing, this great slab of toffee-encrusted dough and sticky currants. Even Pebbie, who normally wolfed down anything that came his way, ate his portion slowly and solemnly, savouring every movement of his packed mouth.

Pebbie was, in fact, the last to finish. We all watched him eat the final morsel, chewing meditatively.

'What do you reckon then?' Tiger addressed his question to Pebbie as though acknowledging his newly acquired status as keeper of the lardy cake.

'How d'you mean?' came the hesitant reply.

'What d'you reckon about *her*?' Tiger jerked his thumb in the direction of the old lady's hedge.

'How d'you mean, reckon?' Pebbie retorted, uneasy at Tiger's changing attitude.

'Reckon,' bawled Tiger. 'Reckon — that's what I mean — *reckon*. Do you reckon she's a *witch*?'

'A witch?' Pebbie quavered, quite unable to cope with this inquisition.

Tiger kicked out at him and then turned to Jess and me: he had put Pebbie in his place.

A slight breeze ruffled the willow leaves above our heads. I remember glancing backwards at the hedge and straining to hear the sound of the harmonium — that would at least mean that the crone was safely engaged. But there was only the summer hum, the squabbling of sparrows, the soft murmur of water.

'I reckon she's a witch.' Tiger — lying back, hands behind his head — waved a foot in Pebbie's direction. 'Marked him didn't she? On his head.'

'What for, Tiger — do you reckon?' Jess paused with clinical interest and then went on dismembering a grasshopper.

'So as she can find him', Tiger dropped his voice and spoke with slow emphasis, '*when his time comes*.'

The phrase was entirely mysterious. It encompassed both birth *and* death; grown-ups used it in hushed tones. For us it simply spelt doom.

Tiger lolled back sucking a bent of grass; Pebbie went pale, clamped the straw hat on his head and glanced over his shoulder. I noticed that his right hand was shaking. It was always that one; the other was quite steady.

'A lure,' Tiger continued. Odd that he should use that word: I suppose things got lured a lot in Ashbourne in those days. 'That's what the lardy cake was, a *lure*.'

'So that she could dab that thing on Pebbie's head', Jess broke in, 'and mark him, like.'

Pebbie's hand was shaking perceptibly as Tiger nodded and sprang to his feet.

'Come on, then,' he growled, 'we better get on.'

The heat beat down as we emerged from our resting place and we broke off some fresh branches, for their shade as well as to keep off the flies on the road that lay before us. It was not really a road, just an ordinary Wiltshire lane, but we knew nothing better: it was the highway to the railway engine.

The road had changed course before we had reached the witch's house and was now heading almost at right angles from the direction it had followed on the first stage of our journey. I suppose that we were now going almost due east.

We straggled along in line, Tiger in front, then Jess and me, followed by Pebbie, Ruth and the little 'un; Tiger's ankles were still fringed with greenery. Screaming swifts skimmed the road ahead of us; I remember the faint smell of clover. The countryside was opening out, the fields — glimpsed between willows and alders — were deep with mowing grass, smudged gold with buttercups and speckled with moon daisies and campions and poppies; a cuckoo was calling close by. The line of the downs now ran on our right, stretching away to distant grey-green headlands to east and west. Ashbourne had dissolved into a fold of the chalkland, only marked by the tiny line of beeches running down the eastern end of the terraced spur of the coombe.

The pollen-laden air was wobbling in the mid-day heat; squadrons of flies spiralled like black smoke above our leafy canopies. The rough cloth of my jacket chafed my skin (we did not wear underwear in those days – I never even had a shirt) and my feet ached.

But I was used to fatigue. Like all the farm children we had to serve our turn – gleaning in the empty fields when the last stook was lifted, pulling weeds, picking up stones, singling mangolds. And if the farmers came to our school, we had to go. They would barge in and just point at us: 'I'll have 'ee' or ''Ee can go, as well.' The teachers never said anything, they just watched. We would be away for days, sometimes for weeks, potato lifting, crow starving or whatever else was wanted – all for a few pennies. It was the same if the Vicar or Mrs Storey-bloody-Ellis came to take one of the older girls into service. No one ever denied them; it was their right to select whom they liked and to throw us back when they had finished with us. Not that we minded. We were glad enough to be shot of the endless chanting of tables, the canings and drill – unless it was very cold or wet. Then we would wear a sack round our shoulders as we worked. Pebbie's brother once caught his hand in the winnowing machine: the farmer swore at him and sent him home with his hand half crushed.

It was probably because it was Chick-Chack Day – and the haymaking had not started – that we could all escape together. We were, in any case, experts at making ourselves scarce if the fit took us and often got walloped for it. I suppose we knew every nook and cranny of the farmyards, watercress beds, hedgerows and open downs; few could pass through Ashbourne in those days without our sharp eyes marking their progress. We once followed the new curate for most of a damp autumn afternoon without his knowing. In the village they still say he was daft because he wore elastic-sided boots and chased butterflies across the downs brandishing a great net above his shovel-hat. He put his hand up Thursa Buckland's skirt that afternoon and, later, we watched him lose a boot in a cottage midden trying to take a short cut back from the watercress beds.

In Ashbourne we were the watchers, the stealthy ones; it was our territory and we could slip unseen from one side of the village to the other if the occasion demanded. But on Chick-Chack Day we were the intruders – and hidden eyes were watching us. Not that we knew. Yet we were uneasy in that flat, lush countryside, especially Pebbie, who kept close to Ruth and the little 'un.

The roadside was alive with birds. Their agitation had preceded us all the way from Ashbourne Mill: the chattering panic of blackbirds, grating calls of pheasants, explosions of partridge wings. Oddly, they were now much fainter and farther ahead, mixed with the distant clatterings of woodpigeons.

Our way curved to the left between tall trees and scattered hawthorns, emblazoned with scarlet instead of the white of Ashbourne. Twice there were quick movements behind blossomed branches: nothing definite, just a tiny scurry in the landscape ahead. No one spoke. We plodded on through the summer hum and occasional cuckoo calls.

Then we saw it clearly: a small dark figure like our own, a good way ahead of us on the left, now in the open running swiftly away, on the other side of neat iron railings – the sort a boy could get through.

We did not clamber through the fence and give chase, as we would instinctively have done in Ashbourne: we were in a strange land and, for us, that small fleeing figure – leaping across thistle clumps and grassy tussocks – spelt danger. It was doing what we knew only too well: carrying tidings of intruders.

Our pace quickened and we drew close together. Ahead were tall elms and the glimpse of a gable end. Then a second house came in sight – and another on our left: both of brick and slate, like the old lady's, so very different from the cottages of Ashbourne with their bulging thatches, like plump tea-cosies dumped down on irregular clunch and flint walls. Further on, to the right, was a clutter of sheds and piled logs, sunk in beds of stinging nettles, with several dark figures lounging at a rough bench before the low slate-roofed building.

'Come on, keep up,' Tiger ordered, mimicking with surprising accuracy the crisp tones of the soldiers who had hauled their guns through the village on the memorable day of the Ashbourne manoeuvres.

It needed all of Tiger's authority to force us on. The little'un, sensing our anxiety, started to snivel; Jess stopped in his tracks. But move forward we did, for Tiger's eyes were blazing and Ruth gave Jess and Pebbie some decisive shoves.

We marched on with Tiger leading. There was a smell of wood smoke, and the gamey whiff of something stewing; on the bench were three dead rabbits, blood oozing from their nostrils; there were guffaws and a banging of pewter mugs.

Standing, grinning down at us, was a tall lanky man in a grubby yellow waistcoat; at his elbow were seated two whiskered ancients in smocks; lounging behind them were three, maybe four, labouring men in tattered shirt-sleeves and a soldier, his scarlet tunic unbuttoned – all with tankards in their fists. Beyond them was a fat woman, hands on hips, and beside her the boy who had spied us from the hawthorns and run ahead across the paddock: he looked warm in his thick jacket. He had a buttoned cap on his fair hair.

We must have been a curious spectacle, a file of weary

children plodding solemnly along at the edge of the road, our wilting branches held aloft like sagging banners.

There were cat calls and snatches of song, mostly from the soldier.

'We're soldiers of the Queen, my lads! All dressed in khaki, going out to fight!'

Then questions were shouted.

'Where're you from, then?'

'Ashbourne dab chicks, are ye?'

'Still feed you on pebble soup up there do they?'

Tiger halted and spun round, his dark face twisted into rage − partly with irritation as Pebbie collided with him.

'Don't matter where we come from or where we're going. We ain't going to hurt nothing,' Tiger shouted.

'Here, you keep a civil tongue in your head − you young devil,' roared back the man in the yellow waist-coat. 'And where d'you reckon you're going anyway − just walking through here as if you owned the place.'

'Off to relieve Ladysmith, as like as not,' called out the soldier.

'No, we ain't,' said Tiger. 'We ain't going to relieve nowhere. We just want to go through.'

'Where to?' demanded the man in the waistcoat. 'And how do we know what you might get up to?'

'We ain't going to get up to anything, Mister,' Tiger blustered. 'We just want to go through.'

'We'll see about that you cheeky young bugger,' replied the man in the waistcoat, bending down to speak to the boy, who nodded and ran off ahead of us into the village. 'Our lads will settle your hash.'

'Better fall back while you're still in good order,' called the soldier.

This was clearly Pebbie's intention. He was already

backing away, I guessed, in preparation for full retreat along the road to Ashbourne; Jess was looking pretty sick and the little'un was still snivelling. My mouth dried and I felt the acid taste of fear; Ruth regarded the scene with sardonic interest.

It was all so public; those moments of indecision before the ale house loungers.

'Better get off back,' said the soldier. 'They're rough little bleeders here, I tell you.'

The fat woman shrieked with laughter. 'Leave 'em alone, Had. It's better'n a pantomime.'

Tiger stood in the road glaring at Pebbie, the bottoms of his trousers now halfway to his ankles. Pebbie's face was glazed with sweat, his straw hat level with his eyebrows.

Tiger took one step towards Pebbie. He looked as though he would kill him. Then an extraordinary thing happened: Tiger shrugged, turned and walked on – and we all followed him. No one spoke – we never did that much anyway – we just walked on amid guffaws and shouts of 'Get off back' and 'Daft little buggers'.

It was a strange place, that village, long and straight with cottages and houses set back behind neat hedges – quite different from the picturesque muddle of Ashbourne nestling in a fold in the downs. There were few signs of life after the crowd at the alehouse, for the dark-suited boy had disappeared again, and all we saw was a donkey tied on a grassy patch and an old lady in white bonnet and apron regarding us suspiciously from her cottage gate. We passed a green painted pump by the roadside, but Tiger wouldn't wait for us to drink.

'Come on', snapped Tiger, 'afore they stop us'.

We had thrown down our branches and, despite the heat and increasing weariness, were doing our best to jog briskly along; Ruth managed to keep up even though she was carrying the little 'un who was grizzling about wanting to go home. I think we had all forgotten the purpose of our journey. There were certainly no thoughts of the railway engine in my head. All I wanted to do was to keep up with Tiger and get out of that awful village. Oddly, it never occurred to me to turn back.

We passed, on our right, some huge iron gates – the like of which we had never seen before – and a gate-house flanked by large stone jars, one of them half-covered with ivy, standing on squat pillars. Then we came to a vast yew hedge, clipped smooth and towering far above our heads, and, beyond, a wooden gate with a small tiled roof over it.

Tiger stopped at the gate. We pressed behind him, peering over at a wide gravel path, bordered by ancient yews, and the low stone tower of a church.

It was a concealed, secret sort of place, enclosed and green; cooling-looking even in the unseasonal heat. Tiger pushed open the gate and walked into the church-yard. It was a bold step, for we had been banished from Ashbourne church. We occasionally played in the churchyard there and on one bitter winter afternoon sought shelter in the porch and then – so cold was the day – within the church itself. There was a large iron stove at the back of the nave and we had huddled round it, gazing up at the soaring arches and the hammer-beamed roof. The vicar caught us there and kicked up a fearful fuss.

'What are you little oiks doing here?' he shouted. It was the first time I was called 'oik'. I suppose it was appropriate.

We scrunched along the gravel path towards the church door. It creaked ominously as Tiger pushed it open, with the clanking of an iron lock. Then there was a chill waft, with a smell of stone that was almost overpowering, as we followed him in. We were standing on a deep, dark blue carpet that stretched away to the other side of the church. There was stillness, broken only by the barely audible squealing of swifts – and now the scent of lilac.

It was too much to comprehend. I just followed Tiger and Jess with the others to the centre of the building, where the carpet crossed, looking towards the altar and a huge maroon-coloured cross with Christ in agony hanging high above the chancel steps. I think we all had our mouths open. It was all so different from the bare little church at Ashbourne; this wonderful carpet, dappled in stained-glass light; shining brass and polished wood; the statue of the Virgin all in blue. I was over-whelmed by feelings of purity and, perhaps more, by the unimaginable luxury of it all.

No one spoke. Pebbie and Jess were gawping up at the crucifix, the little'un had her hands together as if in prayer and Ruth was staring at the Virgin. Tiger was standing by himself. He had not moved from the carpet's crossing.

'Us can bide here awhile,' he called softly. Then he walked forward to the chancel steps, pushing me aside as he did so. He stood there for a full minute – gazing at the altar – raised his arms and then slowly lowered them.

'Us'll be safe in here,' he said, hitching up his sagging trousers, and then began a strange mumbling chant, with the words his father used to call in the cows.

'Cum sah, cum sah – cum sah sah, cum sah sah sah,' Tiger chanted and then turned, his eyes glittering.

'Okus pokus and here us be,' he continued, and then, catching sight of Pebbie, snapped: 'take your hat off.'

Pebbie obeyed. The sight of his blue-stained scalp gave Tiger fresh inspiration.

'One of us have been *marked*,' he intoned. 'Marked for when his time come.'

Pebbie trembled, as Tiger continued his rigmarole with more cow calling, fragments of the Lords Prayer and further references to Pebbie's scalp.

We were kneeling when Tiger finished his litany.

'Oh God, help us get to the railway . . . dum, dum . . . and to smash they village boys.'

Tiger glared down, intoxicated with his power, and then with a dignified wave of his arms assumed a more familiar role.

'Shall us take something? For a trophy, like?'

We shook our heads, in perplexity more than disapproval.

'How do you mean . . .', Pebbie started – and then subsided at a glance from Tiger.

'That'd be stealing,' Ruth protested.

'They'd be *trophies*,' said Tiger. 'You can take things when there's a battle – and things like that.'

'It'd be stealing,' Ruth persisted. But Tiger knew what he wanted. He strode across to the brass eagle which held the bible on its outstretched wings and plucked off the place marker: an elaborately decorated strip of green shot-silk with a long embroidered cross of gold in the middle and twiddly bits at the ends. It was a gorgeous thing and I could see Tiger lusted after it. He draped it across his shoulder and strutted round the chancel, stopping only to examine the figure of a bearded knight in armour lying on his side wearing a painted surcoat.

We were all excited now; even Ruth seemed to have forgotten her outrage at Tiger's theft. It was as though it was our church. That we were conquerors able to take what we wanted.

We started to look round, in case there was anything

40

more to see – or take. Jess was in high spirits and, surprisingly, so was Pebbie, who had replaced his hat, evidently reconciled to Tiger's predictions of doom. We must have been making quite a racket – even the little'un. But we all stopped at Jess's urgent shout and trotted over to the side chapel by the Virgin's statue.

'Look in there . . .' whispered Jess.

The coffin rested on wooden trestles at the centre of the Lady Chapel, partly obscured by a vase of lilies and a shaft of shimmering sunlight.

We had seen coffins before. They were carried through Ashbourne, on a waggon or on men's shoulders, and sometimes rested in the church on the day before a burial. But then they were screwed down. This one was open, the lid leaning against the wall.

Jess and I stepped cautiously into the Chapel. It was bravado on my part: Jess was always drawn to the macabre. The others lingered at the screen.

I got the shock of my life when I looked into the coffin. The skin was wrinkled and sickeningly pale, the colour of dried putty. Just like the face of the crone who had given us the lardy cake.

FOUR

I had snatched only one really good look at the lardy cake woman when she shook me by the neck – but I remembered her face all right: the narrow nostrils and wrinkled skin, the thin, scraggy hair drawn into a tight bun at the back of her wobbly old head; the black dress and lace collar.

When I realised who was in the coffin, I bolted back to Tiger, Pebbie and the girls, crouching in the Virgin's shadow.

'What's up?' Tiger demanded.

'It's the old witch,' I gasped, 'Her as give us the lardy cake.'

'How d'yer mean?' said Pebbie.

'It's her I tell yer.'

'How can her be?'

'Go and look then . . .'

No one moved.

'What d'you reckon?' Tiger turned to Jess.

'How can us've seen her if hers dead?' said Ruth.

Jess ignored this and turned to Tiger. 'Her must've been dead when her give us the lardy.'

'How?'

'Come back to give us it,' Jess replied. 'Come back

from the dead. How many times have anyone give you a lardy?'

Tiger shook his head.

'And her was singing hymns, and her marked Pebbie,' Jess continued. 'On his head . . . so her would know – when his time come.'

Ruth was impressed by this; Pebbie's face was ashen and his hand trembling worse than ever; no one went back to the coffin.

It was then that I spotted the dark figure: standing at the back of the church, close to a pillar. The face was pale; the rest black from top-to-toe. It had so miraculously appeared without so much as the clicking of a lock or the creaking of a door. We were trapped between it and the corpse.

The little'un put her hands together again and one by one we all did the same, including Tiger.

None of us dared look back down the church or at the coffin. There was only the Virgin's enigmatic plaster smile and the faint sounds of the churchyard swifts. I tried desperately not to imagine the old lady slowly sitting up in her coffin or the dark figure floating silently towards us across the blue carpet.

There were rustlings – I imagined the flapping of dark wings – and a footfall close at hand. I did not look. I tried to think of the scent of hay and the brilliant sunlit fields outside; I closed my eyes, but there was only the smell of polish and stone.

Then there was a voice. A man's voice. The words burned into my memory.

'Except ye be converted, and become as little children, ye shall not enter into the kingdom of heaven.'

I opened one eye and saw the hem of a black skirt.

'Whoso shall offend one of these little ones which believe in me . . . '

On and on he went, like Tiger had, but sort of gentle, while we cowered beneath the statue. I remember worrying about the word 'offend': I knew what that meant all right and shut my eye very firmly again.

The next thing I heard was Tiger's voice.

'We only came in here Mister, to sort of rest, like.'

There was a silence, then my arm was gripped and I was lifted up. My eyes were open now and I was prepared to kick and struggle – anything to get away.

'This is marvellous, children – truly marvellous.'

I looked up into a smooth, fresh face and the bluest eyes I had ever seen. He was, I suppose, youngish, maybe twenty-five or so – it's difficult to judge age when you're a child. I noticed that he had big fleshy ears and that his hair was parted in the middle.

'From whence do you come?' he asked.

'How d'you mean,' I gasped, borrowing Pebbie's phrase.

'Where do you come from, child?'

'Ashbourne. We come from Ashbourne.'

'And do you pray there, as well – in the church, I mean?'

'No. We got slung out, like. Reverend Gould said we was oiks.'

'And do you think you are?'

'What?'

'Oiks.'

'I suppose so. That's what he called us.'

The grip tightened on my arm. I feared the worst for I was being shaken – for the second time that morning – and remember wishing that I had not mentioned the business of our being oiks.

'Well, you are not. Indeed you are not.'

He sounded quite cross, but it was not evidently with me.

44

'So that is why you came − to pray for someone who was old. This lady who now lies at rest here?'

'Yes, Mister,' Jess piped up. He seemed quite excited by these goings on. 'We seen her this morning. She sort of come to us up the road − gave us a lardy, and spoke to I and all. And now she's lying here.'

'She appeared to you this morning − in the lane?'

'Yes, Mister,' we chorused − anxious to please, now that it seemed there would be no trouble from this strange man.

He paused and looked at each of us. The little'un began to snivel.

'Do you reckon we could have seen her, Mister?' Jess asked, 'if she was dead, like.'

'Jesus come back from the dead − didn't he Mister?' Ruth added timidly.

'Well ... to the Lord anything is possible − and you may have been his instruments.' He paused again looking straight at Jess. 'Who am I to say? I too am his instrument.'

I think that is what he said, although what it meant I was not exactly sure, but it seemed like confirmation, which was a relief to me. I had begun to have doubts now that everything seemed to be turning out so well. After all, one old lady might be much like another. But evidently it was her, although it seemed odd that this vicar − at least that is what I supposed him to be − should be getting worked up about a witch. I suspected that vicars would not normally get mixed up with broomsticks and black cats and the like. And she had both of those, for I remembered that there had been a besom leaning against the kitchen wall.

But the main thing was that we were not in trouble for being in the church. Even more amazing, I heard the man telling Tiger that he could keep the length of embroidered silk that was still round his neck.

'Let it be a badge,' he said, 'to give you strength in the fight that lies ahead.'

Pebbie butted in here.

'Do you reckon there is going to be a fight, Mister? We was worried there'd be, like.'

'Yes, I am afraid there will – probably many of them – but let this give you strength and the memory of what has happened here today.'

He nodded. I noticed that there were tears in his eyes, and then he knelt down beside us and began to pray until I thought my knees would give out.

When he had finished, he walked with us to a side door of the church. He was not a vicar, he said, but a rector.

The rector told us that he would tell our vicar what had just happened.

'Please don't, Mister,' pleaded Pebbie. 'We'll get a walloping if they know what we been doing.'

'Don't worry about that, young man. Even Gould will sit up when I tell him of what went on here this morning.'

He seemed genuinely sorry to see us go; I felt pretty downcast too, at the prospect of what might happen when we left the church.

The rector stopped at the porch and, to our intense interest, lifted up his skirt to reveal a dark trouser leg and a pocket from which he fished out a sixpenny piece and put it into Tiger's hand.

'This is for you to buy some lemonade on the way back,' he said. Although where he thought we would buy it I had no idea.

Tiger fairly capered down the path in the dappled sunlight.

'A lardy cake *and* sixpence . . . and you haven't pulled your drawers down yet,' he gloated as Ruth picked up the little'un.

'He's a proper daft bloke ain't he,' said Jess.

'Don't matter,' said Tiger, waving his silk band and shaking the sixpence in his hand. 'It don't matter at all. And he was right about the old woman.'

'What we going to do now?' Pebbie demanded.

'Better get on,' said Tiger. 'They boys will be after us afore long.'

The path from the side door led, not to the large gate through which we had come, but to a smaller one in a yew hedge on the other side of the churchyard. As it happened, this was another fortunate turn of events, for it opened into a large meadow with a track leading behind some cottage gardens. It was wonderful that meadow, just ready for cutting, with the grass up to our thighs and spangled with flowers. It was also extremely hot after the cool church.

At the other side of the meadow there was a stile and the path ran on between an apple orchard and a tarred fence. It brought us back on to the village street, some way past the main church gate.

Opposite was an inn – comfortable and thatched – from which came a buzz of voices and occasional murmurs of laughter.

There were boys dotted all along the street: one group was far away, nearly to the pub where the fair-haired lad had spotted us, and another near the church gate.

The group near the church gate was the largest – some five or six boys – and they spotted us as soon as we blundered out into the road from the path across the meadow. On our right were three more, preoccupied with throwing stones up into the branches of a horse chestnut. They had not seen us nor were they aware that their comrades at the church gate were already starting in our direction waving their arms and shaking sticks.

There were only two things we could do. We could either leg it back the way we had come, to hide in the church or in the nearby hedgerows, or we could turn to the right and head for the smaller group to break through them before our pursuers caught up with us.

This was Tiger's dilemma as we stood at the roadside in the centre of that strange village. There was also the problem of what to do with Ruth and the little'un.

Tiger gave them short shrift. 'You get out of the way,' he said to Ruth. 'Take her back to the church and just wait there.'

'No us won't,' retorted my sister. 'Us'll stay together whatever.'

So saying she picked up the little'un, who was brandishing a fistful of buttercups, and headed off down the road to the right, her long skirt flapping, at a very passable speed for a girl carrying a four-year-old. There was nothing for it, but for the rest of us to follow Ruth.

The three boys in our way were trying to bring down birds' nests and it was not until we were some twenty yards off that they saw us coming. But they jumped all right when they realised what was happening: two of them picked up sticks from the foot of the tree and the other started to square up in the middle of the road.

We knocked them flat. Pebbie and I went for the biggest, a powerfully built lad in a smock, and Jess dealt with a skinny youngster who turned tail before we reached them. Tiger had a brief skirmish with the third one, a plump, shock-headed boy, who was quickly dispatched by a passing kick from the little'un as Ruth trotted by carrying her pick-a-back.

The way ahead was now open. But danger lay from behind, for the squad from the church gate was gaining on us and, I seem to remember, the boys from further down the village were also on the move. Our main trouble was Ruth and the little'un: with them, we could not possibly keep ahead.

Our closest pursuers were within a stone's throw of us – and gaining fast – when Tiger turned into a large rickyard which led off to the right.

'Come here – quick,' he shouted. 'We'll get up on one of they.'

We raced across the yard towards the nearest rick. But there was no way we could scale it – and by this time the village boys were pouring through the gate.

'This way – over here,' bawled Jess, running towards an opened rick. There was a ladder leaning against it. It was one of a row of a dozen or so stacks set against the high wall. There was a kind of platform – some seven or eight feet up – where the hay had been cut away. Ruth climbed up to it, followed by Pebbie who pushed the little'un out of the way and then toppled the ladder in his panic as he scrambled on to the platform.

The village boys were now on us and Tiger, Jess and I were trapped in the narrow passage between the ricks with the little'un who was wailing behind us. Tiger ran to the open end brandishing a thatching stick. With its sharpened end it was a dangerous weapon and the first of our pursuers halted abruptly as it whistled under his nose. It was then that Ruth whacked him from above with the handle of a hay-fork. He fell down on the loose hay, screaming and holding his head.

There was a pause and then a great shout from our attackers. Tiger was still waving his stick, his trouser bottoms now well below his knees, the embroidered silk band wound round his neck, with Jess at his side. I was behind them, pushing back the little'un and searching for something to throw.

49

The boys came forward in a rush, but it was difficult for them to get at us as Tiger and Jess backed into the cleft between the ricks with Ruth lashing out at them from above with the hay-fork. Tiger cut one of the boys across the neck with his stick and Ruth got another one on the side of his head. There was a pause and then they came at us again, this time using the ladder as a battering ram. They caught Jess in the stomach with it – he went down holding on to the end of the ladder – just as Tiger fell to the ground wrestling with the lad in the smock whom Pebbie and I had pushed over in our skirmish in the street.

I stepped forward, the ladder buffeting my side, and squared up to the next boy to rush forward: I recognised him instantly. He was the fair-headed one who had spotted us when we had first approached the village.

It was an odd thing to happen in the thick of battle, but I liked the look of that boy as soon as I saw him close to. I think that it was the first time I ever really liked anyone. Before that I had just accepted who ever chanced to come along and then got on with them as best I could. It had never even crossed my mind to consider whether I actually liked Pebbie, Jess and Tiger, or even Ruth for that matter. They were just there. I was never particularly bothered if they were hurt or unhappy. But this boy was different. His face was flushed and ugly with the excitement of the fight. Yet I could tell that he would be fun to be with. He had freckles and wore a flat black cap with an enormous button on top.

He smacked me in the mouth with the flat of his hand and then pushed me over the ladder as I attempted to thump him in the chest. I stood up and tried to grapple with him, but he flung me down over the ladder.

When I struggled to my feet again, he was gone. Two

farm hands, one with a pitchfork in his hand, and a plump woman clutching at her skirts, were chasing them out of the yard.

'You young buggers,' one of the men was shouting.

They went after the village boys, leaving the woman standing over Tiger, Jess and me as we lay tangled up in the ladder. The little'un was howling dismally.

'You naughty children,' she scolded, 'fighting in the master's yard. You ought to be ashamed of yourselves. And look at that poor little mite there, frightened out of her wits she be, poor little soul. And you should be ashamed of yourself, a big girl like you – and what are you doing up there anyway? And where d'you come from anyway? Poor little mite – come to Annie then. Naughty boys that's what you are, just plain naughty.'

On and on she went, while we extracted ourselves from the ladder and then used it to get Ruth and Pebbie down from the rick. I was feeling pretty shaken and so was Jess: he had been nearly squashed flat; Tiger's mouth was beginning to swell. None of us spoke, except for the little'un who began pouring out her troubles. She whispered them into the plump woman's ear and they produced definite responses: 'Oh dear . . . my, my . . . You poor little dear . . . I never did . . . Whatever next . . . the varmints . . . The *railway* . . . just fancy. You poor little mite!'

The little'un kept at it for ages. I think it was the first time that anyone had ever listened to her at all. The woman stopped her at one point and addressed us directly.

'Why you going to the railway for?'

'Business, Missus,' mumbled Tiger, rubbing away at a bruised leg.

She nodded and resumed her one-sided conversation with the little'un. I must give her her due: that plump woman could listen as well as talk. Eventually she stood up, after giving the little'un a hug, and dusted her skirts.

'You better come through here,' she said, taking the little'un by the hand. 'They village boys'll end up on the gallows.'

Whatever the little'un said to the plump woman, it did the trick. She was all over us. She took us to the dairy to wash our faces under the pump – the cold water stung my bruised face – and then let us drink as much milk as we could. We must have drunk gallons; the plump woman said she had never seen anything like it. 'If you don't drown, you'll burst,' she hooted, and called in the dairymaid to witness the remarkable sight.

I was so full that I swear I could feel the liquid slopping about inside me. I found it difficult to walk when the time came to leave. The plump woman accompanied us from the dairy. She led the way, holding the little'un by the hand, across a large lawn and then through an orchard with blossom floating gently down in the warm air. There was a smell of fresh mown grass and the calling of woodpigeons. None of us spoke, we were too full.

'Now you can go through this gate here,' said the plump woman, 'and then alongside this meadow. And keep out of the grass, they'll be cutting here tomorrow. Then you can follow the path on this side of the stream, it'll come out on the road about half a mile on. They village boys will be waiting for ye outside the rickyard, I reckon. So you can get along . . . with your business.' She giggled, and then bent down to give the little'un a hug. 'Bye, bye, my dear – and don't forget what I told ye, now.'

She stood watching us from the orchard gate, waving

to the little'un as we carefully skirted the mowing grass in the shade of a tall hedge.

'Funny lot round here ain't 'em,' Tiger whispered hoarsely, fishing out the green silk band from his pocket and carefully draping it round his neck.

It was all very perplexing, that two grown-ups should behave so uncharacteristically in so short a time. First, the daft clergyman with tears in his eyes and then this extraordinary woman who had allowed us to fill ourselves with milk. In Ashbourne we were always chased away from the dairy door, if we ever tried to hang around there — even the little'un when she appeared towing her lump of wood on its piece of string.

It was really hot now, for the sun was directly overhead and the flies returned in black clouds around our heads. We stopped, after making sure the coast was clear, to pull some branches from the hedge and for Ruth to refill Tiger's boots with fresh grass wrenched from the hedge bottom, before straggling on, as the plump woman had directed, beside the stream, which was more like a weed-filled ditch.

The going was hard now, not only because of the heat and the effects of the milk, but from the knocks we got in the rickyard. Jess was hobbling and complaining about his bruised midriff, Tiger found it very hard to speak as his mouth swelled and I felt desperately tired. We did not have the heart to give Pebbie a thumping for overturning the ladder.

There was also the dreadful possibility that the village boys would fall on us again. If we did not appear from the rickyard gate they would surely guess where we were heading.

But there was no sign of them when we reached the road by a neat wooden stile. The way had curved again and by this time we were well out of the village, the nearest cottage roof was some quarter of a mile back. We moved on as fast as we could, swiping at the flies with the fresh branches. Pebbie was well ahead; his straw hat jammed down, his fat buttocks heaving with exertion.

Odd that we kept going like that, for at that age our moods were as changeable as the downland breezes – unless it was farm work, and then only because we got walloped if we slacked off. It was Tiger who kept us going. Looking back, that too was odd, because there was not a more feckless family in Ashbourne than Tiger's. 'Proper slummocky lot', Father used to call them. Tiger's father was a casual labourer: a sly, raw-boned man; his mother was a harassed, gipsy-looking woman, overwhelmed by pregnancies and beatings. If he wasn't working, Tiger's father used to roam the hedgerows with a mangy old whippet, taking whatever came his way. He never looked anyone in the face. They lived in a tiny ramshackle cottage, like a decaying hay-stack, on the other side of the watercress beds. They never even kept a pig.

Yet Tiger was our leader. There was no doubt about that as we plodded along in the heat. We still had no idea if we could even get to the railway engine, and the plump woman had only laughed when the little'un had told her about it. Not that there was much else we could do but carry on: to turn back would only mean another fight and certain defeat.

So we tramped on behind Pebbie, whose unusual energy had more to do with getting away from the village than enthusiasm for railway engines. He was probably right; the road wound so much that I too began to imagine a pursuing horde behind us at every bend. But there was only the monotonous calling of yellowhammers merging with the summer hum.

Tiger kept stopping to search for dock leaves to put on his injured mouth and the little'un fussed endlessly about going back to see the nice lady.

We rounded yet another bend to find the road empty before us – there was no sign of Pebbie.

'Where's he to, the bugger?' Tiger mumbled out of the corner of his swollen mouth. 'I've had enough of he . . . going to give him what for when I finds him.'

Tiger was in an ugly mood. I could see that from the way his dark eyes narrowed. It had been touch and go whether he went for the little'un when he was looking for dock leaves; I had been tempted to whack her myself, but I had Ruth to contend with and I wasn't sure about her since that jab in the belly.

We found Pebbie sprawled beside the stream, his straw hat on the ground beside him, his head and shoulders buried in tall grass at the top of the bank. We gazed down at him from the bridge.

'What be at?' Jess called.

But there was no reply; Pebbie wiggled his legs as though in some excitement.

Tiger, now beside himself with fury, started off towards the bank just as Pebbie jumped to his feet.

'Snake! Got a grass snake!' Pebbie called, triumphantly holding up a writhing, olive-green creature by the tail.

Tiger stopped dead. The little'un began to crow with interest. 'Becky want – Becky want him'. The snake thrashed furiously, moving its white banded head from side to side and then went limp with its mouth agape. Jess advanced, his eyes shining, but Pebbie pushed him away and jiggled the snake invitingly under Tiger's nose.

It was a whopper, that grass snake. Pebbie was afire with excitement – almost more than he had been about the lardy cake. It was a wonderful moment and Pebbie was going to make the most of it. Not the least to placate Tiger.

The trouble for me was that I loathed snakes; I still do, even grass snakes with their indescribable stink. The thought of touching Pebbie's snake turned me to jelly – as it did Tiger. I had never expected this, but Tiger was scared all right: he went pale as a mushroom. He wouldn't go near the creature. Pebbie obviously thought that this was because Tiger was still angry with him, but the truth slowly dawned, and with it – and even more gradually – the realisation that Tiger had lost his power while Pebbie held that monstrous reptile.

Pebbie draped the animal round his neck – it was still limp with its mouth open – and started off along the road with a jaunty step, closely pursued by the little'un calling, 'Want him, want him'. I followed behind Tiger, leaving Ruth and Jess to bring up the rear. Occasionally Pebbie would stop, and would wave the snake above his head; it was now slowly coiling and re-coiling, and Tiger and I kept our distance.

Pebbie did not overdo this unexpected ascendancy. He was a cautious and apprehensive boy, who knew only too well the reverses of fortune. Like Tiger's family, the Titcombes were a slummocky lot. They had one of the best cottages in Ashbourne, at the top of the village with a good-sized garden, sheltered under the downs and full of ancient apple and greengage trees. It had been left to run down after Pebbie's mother died. His father had since married a fat widow from Liddington way, who was lackadaisical, never bore him children and spoke always with a sort of suppressed anger. Pebbie's mother was consumptive and had been more than a year dying. When he was younger he used to cry a lot at school; we would stand round looking at him with mild interest. He used to keep newts in an old copper boiler, but they always escaped. After a row with his elder brother, he found that his jackdaw had had its neck wrung.

He had a passion for animals. The snake was nearly five-foot long and it meant more to him than just a means to keep Tiger at bay. By now it was becoming very active and, during one of Pebbie's displays of how to handle a snake, it voided a dark-brown liquid, including a half-digested frog, over his jacket. The stench was appalling; the little'un ran back to Ruth; but Pebbie was happy enough, caressing and talking to the creature.

'Better look out for some frogs for his dinner,' Pebbie crooned. 'I'll call him King. That's a good name for a snake, King.'

Tiger groaned and plodded on, holding a dock leaf to his mouth with one hand and his branch aloft with the other.

The combined smell of Pebbie and King was colossal: it was worse than a dead horse in a midden. We got the full benefit when we stopped to cool off in the tall grass and the cow parsley. Pebbie would keep sidling up to exhibit some of the snake's more remarkable attributes.

'Look here,' he would say, 'he's got black and white spots on his belly.' He was fascinated by the creature's flickering tongue. 'He don't half hiss if you squeeze him.'

'How do you know he's a he?' Ruth interjected. 'Her could be a her.'

'He's too big for a her — ain't ye, King?' said Pebbie, quite wrongly as I now realise — King was probably a Queen. 'He's a King, right enough,' he crowed, waving the snake at Tiger in a convivial way.

And, in a way, Pebbie was right, for King dominated us: he subdued Tiger, excited the little'un, fascinated

Jess – repelled me – and Pebbie was his acolyte. Only Ruth seemed untouched by the reptile. I was conscious of it all the time, of its stench and its gimlet eyes, and the sinister swaying of its flat head. Tiger's gold-embroidered band paled into insignificance beside this.

'You ought to put King in water,' said Jess.

'What, to sort of baptise him, like?' asked Pebbie.

'No, to wash him. He do smell terrible.'

Pebbie was clearly taken with the idea and jiggled King contentedly by the tail as we got up to walk on again. Yet I feared that his contentment would be short-lived, for I saw on Tiger's face such a look of hatred as I'd never seen before.

FIVE

Across the fields we could hear the church bell, faint but distinct. It had a deep note. It was the kind that was tolled when the old ones died in the villages in those days.

'That's for the old witch,' hissed Jess. 'They be burying her now.'

'Do you reckon her'll come back — when hers buried, like?' Pebbie whispered. He looked worried again, and shifted King across his shoulder.

'You don't half talk daft, you lot,' Ruth said, uneasily.

There was nothing in sight, just the empty road curving away into the heat haze. My feet were aching. I would not have admitted this — not in boots made by Jimmie Bunce — but they rubbed my ankles and I could feel every stone through the soles. Jess was flagging too. So was Ruth. Only Pebbie was still briskly stepping it out, followed at a safe distance doggedly by Tiger.

We were still in line like soldiers. We marched in file to Acorn Bridge because that was the proper thing to do. If we had had a Union Jack we would have flourished it bravely for Lord Roberts.

Our heads were full of rubbish in those days.

Later in the afternoon we came to a cottage entirely

covered with ivy. You could tell it was a cottage from the shape, but I was afraid at what might lie inside. Jess started on about Red Indians, and I imagined them creeping across the fields toward us.

A disembodied voice floated from the hedge to our right, and we all jumped.

'Where you young 'uns going, then?'

An old man, or so he seemed, with a great bushy beard and long white hair was sprawling in the shade of the hedge bottom. His stick was planted in the ground with a straw hat on the end. At his side was a rough canvas bag, the sort that could be carried over your shoulder. A filthy bandanna handkerchief protruded from beneath his beard, and he had dark glittering eyes.

'Come far have ye?'

We gaped at him.

'Ashbourne,' Ruth replied.

He nodded amiably enough. At least there were no sarcastic remarks about pebble soup.

'You a tramp, Mister?' Jess asked.

The old man nodded again, heaving himself up on one elbow as he did so.

'Have you come far, Mister?' Jess continued.

'Suffolk – that's about as far as I go – but I come from round here. Usually walk through about this time.' He plucked a bent of grass and chewed, gazing thoughtfully at King.

'He's a big'un ain't he?'

The old man pushed himself up to a sitting position.

'You heard the bell?'

We nodded.

'That's for an old 'un gone – the big bell. They always use the big one for an old 'un. Parson must have made a mistake.'

'How do you mean – "mistake"?' asked Jess.

60

'That's what they say around here. When the parson makes a mistake in the prayers – someone goes.'

'How do you mean, Mister – "goes"?'

'Goes. Passes on, like. Dies. When the parson makes a mistake reading the prayers.'

'Coo, that'd be like murder,' gasped Jess. 'Do you believe it, Mister?'

'Don't matter what I believe.'

'Why not, Mister?'

'Cause it don't. If that's what they believe, then that's all that matters for they.'

'You don't believe in witches do you, Mister?' chimed in Ruth.

'That all depends on what you means by a witch,' the old man chuckled. 'I dare say that one could bide in that old ivy cottage yonder.'

And then he told us the story of Wat Sannell's ride to Highworth, as we stood looking down at him.

Wat was a young harum-scarum in olden days. He scoffed at two gaffers because they believed Moll Phillips supped with the devil in her cottage and said she would be burnt alive in Highworth market place. But Wat Sannell didn't care. He pulled up the giant thistle she was supposed to dance round at night. Then he shot Moll Phillips's black cat with his master's birding-piece, and the poor creature jumped as high as the cottage and fell dead at its mistress's door. When she spied Wat, she swore vengeance against him.

'Thee bist a very cruel fellow', said the tramp, pretending to be one of the gaffers, 'and Moll will pay thee off'.

Then he told us how Wat, who was a serving lad at the Manor House, took himself off to Highworth to buy a pair of silver hawk-bells for his master's daughter, Mistress Dorothy. He found a few coins left in his purse, so he swaggered off to the inn and drank several pots of double beer. There was thunder rumbling over the downs when he rode out of Highworth market square.

Not far out of town he came on a woman sitting on a stone by the road side, with her face turned away. Wat jumped down and walked towards her.

The tramp put on his best voice, which he used for Wat Sannell, 'My pretty maid, you must be lonely here awaiting for your lover.'

So saying, Wat bent down to remove her wimple, and received a violent blow from behind which shot him head over heels on the grass. When he scrambled to his feet, swearing, he found the maid clean gone and no one in sight.

The old tramp paused, grinning, and beckoned us to sit down beside him in the long grass in the shade of the hedge.

Then he went on to tell us how Wat Sannell recaptured his horse and was thrown to the ground by the saddle slipping beneath him. He heard a fearful chuckle behind him, but there was no one to be seen. Worse, he discovered that he had taken the wrong way: a flash of lightning showed him a gibbet with the remains of a corpse hanging in chains.

Jess was leaning against me and I felt him shiver.

The old man's voice rose as he related how Wat Sannell found the right road at last, but he had gone less than a hundred yards when a great black cat with flaming eyes appeared and sprang on to the horse's neck and flung him to the ground. The horse dashed away and was never seen again.

Later that night Wat Sannell appeared at the door of the village smithy, bruised and bleeding. He shouted, 'Give me your matchlock,' pushing the blacksmith aside, and grabbed the weapon from the wall. 'Now,

witch,' he bawled, 'we shall see who has the mastery.'
Then he took the silver hawk-bells from his pouch and
crushed them with terrible force between his teeth and
rammed them into the barrel of the matchlock. 'Lead
will not kill thee, but *silver* will send thee to thy master.'

He rushed out of the smithy and down the road to
Moll Phillips's lonely cottage. Through the gloom he
saw the eyes of a cat.

'Now I have thee,' Wat cried and fired the gun with a
deafening bang. But the animal disappeared and Wat
Sannell fell to the ground, groaning and quivering as
though in a fit.

'Next morning', said the tramp slowly, 'they found
Moll Phillips in her cottage, slain by gun-shot wounds
with the gurt cat mewing over her mistress's corpse.'

There was a long silence after the old man finished.

Then Jess said, 'Was that her cottage as we just passed?'

'Might be,' the tramp said.

Again we were silent and the insects hummed. Ruth
was the next to speak.

'He just got drunk and murdered her, didn't he, Mister?'

The old man fished out a clay pipe from his pocket.

'Well, you seen the cottage — and no one have lived
there since I don't know when.'

Even King had remained quiet while the tramp told
his story. But now the creature writhed and coiled again
on Pebbie's shoulder as Ruth jumped to her feet and
picked up the little'un in her arms.

'Where do this road go then, Mister? We ain't exactly
sure, like.'

'Highworth,' came the reply. 'This road do go to
Highworth.'

'What's hawk-bells for?' said Jess, after we had been walking for a few minutes.

No one answered. The road was straighter now and passed through more open country.

We were all subdued — except King, who was restless. I had never heard a grown-up tell a story like that. He did it very well: I nearly yelled when he went on about the cat and the corpse on the gibbet.

Jess loved it. He was never so happy as when he was scared stiff by ghosts. His father was nearly as bad. Sluggie Bunce was a shepherd; a cheerful, square-built man with a broad, weather-beaten face who, unlike most shepherds, was sociable and almost garrulous. In the lambing season he lived most of the time up on the downs, in a tall wooden caravan with tiny high windows and skylarks singing overhead. It was painted green and had small iron wheels. If he wasn't talking of sheep, or his spuds, he would yarn about strange goings-on around Ashbourne Down. Every natural feature had some weird attribute: the dew pond where the water was always green after a horse-riding actress from Lambourne had drowned herself in it, or the queer pile of sarsen stones which he called the Devil's Den, though no one else did. My father said he was off his head from being by himself so much with the sheep. Jess's mother, a buxom woman with short reddish hair and a sweet smile, was also superstitious and possessed an encyclopaedic knowledge of herbs and cure-alls. Mother swore that Sluggie was not Jess's father.

I decided to take the tramp's tale with a pinch of salt. It was different from the business with the old lardy cake woman: that was religious, like Jesus coming back from the dead and the parson making mistakes in the prayers. But I was uneasy at being on the road to Highworth — and so was Jess: he'd swallowed the whole story, flaming cats and all. Ruth was unconcerned and the little'un did not seem bothered; Pebbie was talking to King and Tiger was looking daggers at both of them.

Ahead of us was what looked like a farmhouse; a large one, with a slate roof and thatched barns and a scattering of outbuildings above hedges of may blossom. It was the first we had passed since leaving the village.

Warily, we approached a white wicket gate set in a low flint wall. We knew we would get short shrift if we got in the way − kicked in the backside or squashed by a shirehorse.

We could see no one. There was just a smell of lilac and a straight brick path leading between box hedges and old-fashioned flower beds to a green front door. Further on, a five-barred gate had swung open. There were none of the familiar farm sounds − only the noise of squabbling sparrows in the empty rickyard.

Pebbie draped King's nasty little head over the flint wall so that he could see better.

The farmhouse was tall and built of stone with large windows, pointed like in a church and edged in yellow bricks. It couldn't have been all that old, but every window we looked in revealed only bare, dusty floorboards and a gaunt empty kitchen. The place was deserted: not a chair or table, nor plough, waggon or animal to be seen.

We felt our spirits rise again with the sense of power that we had experienced in the church − as if the place was ours. Tiger broke a window in the stable with a broken axe handle that he found in some stinging nettles, but we couldn't climb in because of the bars; Jess pulled off a pipe from a water-butt and the water poured noisily over the kitchen yard. We ran into the front garden and I kicked over a stone vase with some ferns in it, while Tiger flung stones at the bedroom windows.

Even the little'un uprooted flowers, while Pebbie watched. Ruth looked on with the same half-amused expression on her face.

Our destructive frenzy died away and we stood gazing up at the gaunt, empty house. I expected a dark figure to appear in one of the upstairs windows looking down at us.

It was then that I smelled King very close at hand, and heard Pebbie whispering.

'Here, will you hold King? I wants to have a piss, like.'

I jumped back. Nothing would have made me touch King. But I could understand Pebbie's predicament. We must have drunk gallons of milk, but unlike the rest of us poor Pebbie had a difficulty. His mother had sewn up his fly-buttons when she was cutting down his father's old trousers, and he could not have removed his jacket and braces while hanging on to King who, like the rest of us, was hot and consequently very active.

Desperately, Pebbie shoved King into the arms of the little'un and went off behind a privet hedge. He wouldn't normally have done that. We thoroughly enjoyed convivial piddling contests, rivalling each other in altitude and trajectory, but the presence of Ruth and the little'un had prevented that.

When Pebbie strolled back from behind the hedge, Tiger was waiting for him. Pebbie had his hat off and was scratching his scabs. Tiger went for him like a lunatic. The snake began to writhe and convulse as if it would strangle the little'un. Like Pebbie, she roared with fright.

Pebbie went down under the charge. He made no attempt to fight back, but just let Tiger sit on his chest, grip his ears and bang his head on the ground. Luckily for Pebbie, he was lying on grass or Tiger would have split his head open.

66

Jess and I stood and watched Tiger's revenge, ignoring my small sister's screams of panic from under the snake.

Ruth had been at the other side of the garden when Tiger launched his attack. I had forgotten about her altogether in the excitement of the moment. She suddenly ran past me, holding her black skirt nearly up to her knees. She got the snake away from the little'un in a jiffy. King knew who was master: he went limp again and let his mouth fall wide open.

Without a word Ruth strode across to Tiger and struck King's head in his face. That did the trick. Tiger was half way across the garden before I had time to collect my wits.

Tiger retreated through the wicket gate and stood in the road looking back at us, while Ruth threatened him with the snake. Pebbie lay on the grass for a little and then struggled to his feet. He searched for his straw hat in a flower bed, while Ruth waited, holding the limp snake in her right hand. She gave him back to Pebbie and then went over to the little'un, who had stopped screaming.

It took both King and Pebbie some time to recover from the fight in the garden. The farmhouse was obscured by distant roadside elms before King thought it safe to begin writhing again on Pebbie's shoulder as we continued along the Highworth Road.

SIX

Ruth's interference in the fight was the first I had ever seen in our childish disputes. Before, we just stood by and watched. It was usually Pebbie who would be getting it – from Tiger or Jess or me – although Jess and I would sometimes tussle, and Tiger went for either of us when the fit took him.

I am very sorry, because of what happened later, that I did not stick up for Pebbie sometimes. I bullied him when I felt like it in those days. The trouble was that he was fat and slow on the uptake – 'dummel' as we used to say – and just wouldn't stick up for himself. He always had something wrong with him, usually impetigo, and he stank. Not that this was unusual; we never bathed in those days, except on really hot summer days when we occasionally swam in the mill pool. It was just that Pebbie's smell was different. Tiger had a rancid, almost acid sort of smell and Jess a lighter, floury one. God knows what I smelled like, but Pebbie's was broader and more comprehensive than that of anyone I have known. It's a funny thing, but I cannot recall Ruth smelling at all. The little'un did, but not Ruth: somewhere she must have found a place to wash, or mop herself down. It could not have been easy with the three of us – and our parents – sleeping in two small upstairs rooms and only a bucket to carry the water up from the pump or, if that broke, from the stream. Ruth was a fastidious, secret sort of girl; I only once saw her enter the earth closet at the end of our garden. I am still not sure why she came on the walk to Acorn Bridge. It was certainly not to look after me, as she had told Tiger. I suppose, like us, she just wanted to. Although she couldn't have known what we intended when she spotted us in our excitement running down from the coombe.

As we tramped in Wat Sannell's footsteps, I thought of the boy I had fought with in the rickyard; I had not really noticed much about him in the heat of the fight. He certainly did not smell particularly. Then there was our madness at the empty farmhouse: I wondered whether we would catch it for what we had done. Looking back, it was strange that we should have come across that farm on that particular day.

The flies came at us worse than ever in the open countryside, there were cows in every field, and I heard a faint drawn-out rumbling through their hum. It was different from the distant boomings we'd heard earlier on.

We seemed to lose all sense of purpose after Tiger's savagery and the aimless riot at the farmhouse. I was tired and hot and really couldn't think clearly any more. Pebbie was lagging behind, I could hear him sobbing and slobbering, and the little'un was tottering along by herself, grumbling about that nasty thing. Ruth and Jess were walking together. Tiger was in front, swiping at the clouds of flies with his branch. The lush countryside had dwindled to scraggy fields, covered with thistles and dry cow-pats. I was homesick for Ashbourne, longing for chalk soil and open downland. Oddly, and for the first time, I felt sorry for Pebbie; only a little, and not for long. Ruth had shamed me, I suppose. Yet afterwards I bullied him again and stole his fish hooks and let his newts out. The funny thing is he once told me that I was the only one who hadn't bullied him. Poor old Pebbie: that was just what he wanted to believe.

I'll say this for Pebbie, though: he was resilient. Even after the worst of Tiger's drubbings he would bounce back. He did it after the fight at the farmhouse.

'How long d'you reckon it'll be, like', I heard him say from behind as he walked on, 'before we gets to the engine?'

'Don't know,' growled Jess.

'It'll be like a gurt cannon on a wooden carriage,' replied Pebbie, stepping it out to keep up with us. 'That's what I reckon.'

I was almost in a trance by this time, just moving my feet mechanically forward with no hope of seeing anything but the endless, empty road. But at least there were trees ahead – they looked like osiers – and, behind them, a line of beeches.

It was Tiger who spotted the bridge. He stopped, turned, and then waved and pointed ahead, now in his role of good old Tiger who would take us to see what we had come to see. Like Pebbie, he too could bounce back. There was no trace of the vanquished bully in him now. Not that you could vanquish Tiger, he just kept coming at you – or assumed another guise.

The grass became lusher and hedgerows returned as we headed on towards the bridge. It looked a big one by our modest standards, certainly larger than the one over the mill race at Ashbourne and the ones which crossed the winding stream that had accompanied us for most of the way from the village. It was much more humpy than those: just what you would need to get an engine under.

It was brick and modern looking; there was a crow standing, black, and somehow menacing, on its stone coping. Great tits were busy in the hedges and a yellowhammer started up on our right. 'A little bit a bread and no cheeeese,' Jess shouted exultantly, imitating its song.

Marco Polo approaching the forbidden city could not have been more excited than we were at that moment.

Ruth started to trot. 'Us don't want to miss it going under the bridge,' she called back to us.

Soon, we were all trotting, leaving the little'un behind. King must have been quite shaken about, the rate his head was bouncing around as Pebbie rolled along beside us. Tiger was grinning to himself with a secret look of satisfaction.

Ruth reached the bridge first, followed by Tiger and then Jess and me.

'Where is it then?' Jess exploded as we jumped up, our feet kicking, looking down over the parapet at a long stretch of water − straight as a die, but weedy at the edges.

'Funny sort of river, that,' said Jess.

That such an apparently natural feature should run straight was a paradox for anyone from Ashbourne, where everything curved and nothing was straight.

'That's the Wilts and Berks Canal,' said Pebbie. 'Runs up to Abingdon it do.'

We gaped at Pebbie as he carefully rearranged King across his shoulders.

The Wilts and Berks Canal was already sagging into disrepair, but for us it was a great discovery. We scrambled down to it from the other side of the bridge − all thoughts of the railway engine scattered.

It was a long green vista: a straight, secret stretch of water − dark, almost sinister, fringed with rushes and yellow flags. Behind were osiers, in marshy ground, and behind them a high, level bank lined with beeches. There was the turquoise flash of a kingfisher above the dark water and the jerky semaphore movements of a wagtail feeding at the water margin.

It was all so strange; we hardly knew what to do. Tiger stood at the canal edge whacking a curved stick against his leg, watching a swimming water vole. Ruth was squelching about in the osiers with the little'un. In the distance a dog was barking.

Jess was standing with Pebbie, stroking the snake's tail.

'Why don't you give King his wash?' Jess asked. 'He don't half stink.'

Pebbie considered the matter.

'Ah,' he said. 'I been thinking about that . . . I been thinking I'd better.'

'Go on then – put him in,' Jess said encouragingly.

Pebbie knelt down and very gingerly lowered the huge snake into a clear patch of water beside clumps of flags. He held him behind the head; King immediately began to make swimming movements, throwing his body into vigorous S-shaped waves.

'Look at him! Look at him!' Pebbie shouted with delight.

Tiger strolled along the bank, and in a single vicious movement brought his stick down on King's head, slashing Pebbie's hand as he did so.

Several things happened at once. Pebbie roared in pain and King swam majestically away, driving a flotilla of whirligig beetles frantic. Ruth screeched, 'You cruel bugger', and sprinted from the osiers, just as Pebbie stood up, as if – for once in his life – he had been going to square up to Tiger.

Ruth caught Tiger completely unawares, from the

72

side. It was a good shove. Tiger toppled slowly side-
ways into the dark water beside the yellow flags, while
Pebbie wept. The snake vanished into a clump of reeds
on the opposite bank.

Then I heard a growing rumbling noise. A moment
later, there was a massive blast of sound.

Behind us, on the high bank, was the railway engine.
A great, dark-green cylinder with a brass dome on top,
and smoke dragged horizontally backwards from its tall
funnel. A huge middle wheel and a long green tender.
The noise smashed down at us. We gaped up at the
hissing and crashing monster: Tiger, with the water
nearly up to his neck and the silk band floating beside
him; Pebbie, tears streaking his dirty cheeks; Ruth, arms
akimbo, standing with Jess and me on the canal bank;
the little'un transfixed among the osiers.

None of us moved until the last carriage had disappeared behind the beeches to our left and the clattering
of the wheels had died.

PART TWO

The Works

SEVEN

I was thirteen when I next trudged along the road through Liddiard Parva on a damp October morning. It still seemed a long way, although nothing like the haul on Chick-Chack Day four years before.

I woke long before dawn to the shrieking of barn owls on the dark slopes of the coombe high above the cottage. There was a drip of water from the thatch into the rainwater tub beneath our squint dormer window and the steady breathing of Ruth and Becky from the darkness on the other side of the room.

I dozed and woke again to candle glow and a looming shadow on the low, lime-washed ceiling.

'Come on young'un, time to be getting out,' Father whispered gruffly.

He put his hand on my shoulder and rocked me vigorously until I propped myself up on my elbows. There was a whiff of stale sweat and the faint smell of horses.

'It's your big day, today, mind. Mustn't be late. Got to be spry for the factory.'

Oddly, I sensed a feeling of guilt in this hard, gruff man as he spoke again – quite softly, for him – so as not to wake my sisters.

'I've told your mother to put out some water for you to wash in . . . '

His voice trailed off at this improbability as he placed the candle-holder carefully on the sacking beside my mattress. He groped his way back to the shabby curtain, behind which I could hear Mother moving about.

There was no bowl on the kitchen table when I came back from the privy. But Mother was up by then, standing in the lamplight by the stove. She did not speak – she was going a bit queer by then, I later realised – but she was cooking fried bread and black pudding for me that morning. There was one of Father's Ellison's pippins laid on a clean red and white spotted hand-kerchief with a hunk of bread and a lump of farm cheese, which we got cheap when it was spoiled.

Mother gave me a sad smile, as I walked out from the lamplight into the misty darkness. Father came with me as far as our gate.

'You'll be able to get a proper wage now,' he growled. There was nothing I could say, for I had my own worries that morning, but I knew he was still troubled at taking me away from the farm. Mr Thorne had picked Jess and me from school for mangold sing-ling. He just walked into the classroom, as usual, and took us out and, that time, I never went back. Not that I worried. I hated school and Mr Thorne said he was pleased with me. He was not a bad master, but he was a hard one of the old breed. He always wore the same clothes, summer and winter – short dust-coat, tweed cap, breeches and leather gaiters – and he clung on to every farthing. In the end, Father stuck up to him.

'You'll have to pay him a proper wage, Mr Thorne,' he said. 'He's getting a big lad, now.'

But old Thorne never paid more than a few coppers he had in his pocket and I never made above a couple of shillings a week. And that was why Father took me away, even though he had been with Mr Thorne all his life and our cottage belonged to the farm.

Father had arranged that Abel Goddard and Jack Ball should take me into the Railway Works. They had been there for best part of a year and were supposed to be making good money.

Abel and Jack — hulking louts of about fifteen, I suppose — were waiting for me at the end of the lane. They had filled their pockets with mushrooms and blewits, for their mates at work they told me. Even then, I sensed that they were doing it to curry favour; that country people might need to do such things. They told me that I had to call them 'Bodger' and 'Stiffy', those were their names in the Works.

We made poor time that morning, for the mist thickened in the valley, muffling our voices and obscuring any sign of dawn. I stumbled along, for what seemed like eternity, behind the feeble glow of Stiffy's lantern worrying about having 'G.W.R.' branded on my backside, as Bodger swore I should on my first day in the Works.

There was a lightening of the gloom as we reached Liddiard: dim trees and a barn-gable took shape, towering far above us. A huge horse and then its cart loomed out of the mist, both strangely magnified with the three gigantic figures sitting like grey statues on bundles of straw. A dog was barking close by; there was the smell of cattle and then angry shouts from the cart.

'Come on, Stiffy. Blast it, wur'st tha' been?'

'Climb up smartish — you lazy young buggers.'

'T'will be breakfast-time afore us makes a start at this rate.'

We clambered aboard and the cart lurched forward. No one spoke, not even Bodger. There was only a squeaking of wheels, a jingling of harness and the blowing of the horse. The road climbed from the village – nothing like on the downs, just a gentle slope – but it was sufficient to reveal the eastern sky reddening, tinting the blanket of mist below us.

There was a subdued twittering of linnets in the half light, and then a bellowing which boomed and echoed over the sleeping countryside. It lasted for several seconds before dying down into a prolonged moan.

No one moved or said anything; the horse plodded on, puffing and snorting, between straggling houses of red brick and slate like the old crone's at Liddiard.

I had occasionally heard the factory hooter from the downs at Ashbourne – faint and distant – when the wind was from the north-west, yet I was unprepared for its closer impact: a place that could produce a din like that might easily brand your backside.

There was no one in sight on the outskirts of the town, but plumes of smoke were drifting from chimney-pots into the damp morning air. Further in, misty cones of light illuminated street after street of identical, slate-roofed houses; a few of the shops were already lit with the harsh glare of what I guessed was electric light.

The horse turned, without the need for reining, through open wooden gates and then on into a wide yard, fenced with creosoted railway sleepers and with a solitary laburnum tree in one corner. We halted beside a mountain of coal. Sacks were filled with coal and loaded on the waggon while our small cargo of straw and some sacks of potatoes were taken off. We all lent a hand, working as if the Devil was after us.

The second blast of the hooter came as we laboured: louder than ever at such close range.

The scene was transformed when we drove out from

the merchant's yard. Now the streets were full. On all sides, from every side turning, came dark figures, hurrying along – all in the same direction. There were no greetings, no one spoke; an army of men tramping along, in greasy caps and lead-grey clothes, their expressions tense as though driven towards some grim ordeal; the pavements echoed to the crunching tread of their boots.

There were thousands of them. An ocean of men as far as I could see. And still they kept coming on, pouring into the shuttered, lamp-lit streets; their faces pale and intent: a few smudged with the grime of the day before. We rode through them on our laden waggon. Several glanced up at us with something like hatred in their faces.

It was a frightening business that first approach to the Railway Factory. I had, by that time, been to the town on market day on more than one occasion and to Marlborough Mop – and once to Highworth Michaelmas Fair – but the crowds then had been nothing like the grim cohorts of that October dawn. I saw men like that in Flanders as we were moving up the line to Neuve Chapelle. Then, too, I had not known what to expect, and that was what upset me as I sat there on old Sammy Boulton's cart.

The hooter bellowed a third time as we reached the factory wall; this time the horse reared in fright, but still the crowd came on oblivious of her flying hooves. My companions jumped down from the waggon. One of the Liddiard men stopped and looked up at me.

'Come on, young'un,' he called 'you get off here and all.'

His bronzed country face was comforting in that

buffeting throng. He took my arm and shoved me along towards two huge brown-painted doors, opened to reveal a dark tunnel into which the workmen were pouring like a flood.

'Now bide you here,' said the Liddiard man. 'By breakfast time a gaffer will come by. Then you says "Chance of a job, sir?" – and don't act cheeky or you won't get nothing.'

'And if you gets took on us'll burn your arse for ye,' Bodger shouted as he headed into the tunnel gloom.

I pressed back against the factory wall, feeling its granite roughness through my corduroy jacket. There was a faint taste of smoke and oil in my mouth. If anything, the press of men increased. They were hurrying more than before, some hatless with unlaced boots and shirts unbuttoned; a grubby-faced lad of about my age came trotting by, jacket and waistcoat over his arm, his face puckered in anguish.

The hooter sounded a fourth time, with two mighty blasts that shook the factory wall behind me. Within seconds, the great doors were slammed shut and the street was empty, save for a few solitary running figures, a few hopefuls lounging at the tunnel entrance and the now distant waggon that had brought us in from Liddiard.

As I later discovered, there were dozens of foremen in the Works; it was purely a matter of chance which one passed by that decided the shop in which a man could labour for the rest of his working life. Yet for a raw country clodpole that morning, the 'Gaffer' was the lord of the whole vast factory, with charge of thousands upon thousands of lives: I waited for the doors to swing open to reveal him. But they stayed shut. There was only a steady trickle of men, walking or sauntering – some with newspapers under their arms – through a smaller door to the right of the tunnel entrance.

One of them, a stocky neat man with a pink scrubbed face, stopped and then turned, as though as an after-thought. He had glanced at me when he walked by and I had dropped my gaze.

'Do you want a job, boy?'

He addressed me directly, across the heads of the waiting men and a couple of town boys.

'Country lad, ain't you?' He spoke again, removing his bowler hat and scratching his grizzled head, before I could answer. I nodded, hardly knowing what I was doing, but noticing his intense eyes and the enormous hands, one of which hung in the air – as if suspended by an invisible thread – beckoning to me.

'You'd better come along,' he said. 'I need another boy.'

That is how I started work in 13 Shop, 'the frame shed', with Mr Johnson as my gaffer. It was typical of him that he chose me like that; no unnecessary talk, just a shrewd glance and a quick decision.

I was set to work as soon as I had been taken to the Works doctor by a fierce office boy who repeatedly kicked me on the ankles. In the manager's department I signed what was to be my copy of the *Rules & Regulations of the Great Western Railway* and collected my brass check.

'Can you read?' the office boy asked contemptuously. I nodded and then shook my head in confusion.

'Give it here,' he snarled, snatching the brown booklet from me, and proceeded to recite, slowly and with some difficulty, apparently reading at whim: 'Any workman absent through lead poisoning must at once inform his Foreman. Any workman found playing, idling or quarrelling during working hours will be liable to a fine of two shillings and sixpence. Any workman who goes into a workshop in which he is not usually employed without proper authority before the hooter sounds, or washes his hands in oil, will be liable to a fine of one shilling . . . '

He went on and on until he got tired of the charade and flicked to the last page.

'I, the undersigned, having been appointed as a Boy . . . etcetera, do hereby bind myself to obey the foregoing rules and regulations.'

He paused and glared at me.

'Got to do this *if ye can't read*,' he said and then continued: 'As witness my hand this eleventh day of October nineteen hundred and four . . . signed J. Clack.'

He threw the book at me.

'What sort of name's that?' he hooted. 'Clack! They'll stop your clack in No. 13 Shop. Proper little buggers they are there.'

Then he marched off, leaving me to follow him between gaunt stone buildings and lines of railway waggons.

The frame shed was overwhelming. I could never have conceived of such a place. It was so big I couldn't see the other end and the noise smote at the stomach and tore at the ears: a frantic din of hammering, the hissing of steam, and the clanging and shrieking of drills, saws and slotting machines. Overhead, there were great whirling wheels, long lines of shafting and loose flapping belts. The sound pressed against me as I walked between rows of half-built waggons and carriages to the forges. In the heat of that place I toiled for the next year. It was my job to heat the rivets and do anything else that was required – from fetching buckets of water to holding a nail bag in front of rivet heads that were being cut away, to prevent fragments flying in the workman's face. The forge work was the worst. The fires seared my eyes and scorched my cheeks as I tended the rivets; I had to drop them into rows of holes drilled in a sheet of iron and then place them over the hot coals. There was a constant pushing and shoving with the other rivet boys for the best position at the fire.

The first day was hell. My grub was stolen and my cap kicked half the length of the frame shed; I was sent off to ask innocently for a 'toe punch' and got booted for my trouble. No one burned my backside, but I was half drowned in a bosh of dirty water by the other rivet boys – all of them townees – who made no secret of their contempt for yokels.

In the end, I went for the worst of them: a small, barrel-chested lad with a sallow, pox-pitted face who wore tied round his throat the red spotted handkerchief which Mother had so carefully ironed and wrapped my food in before dawn. I was half crazed by the noise and goaded beyond despair by that boy's sneering face. I punched him on the nose before he even realised my desperation; I hit him in the face again and I was doing my best to break his ribs before they pulled me away.

I was kicked again, this time by the chargehand. I was trembling so much I could hardly drop the rivets into their holes, let alone jostle for a place at the forge.

They came for me after the dinner-time hooter had sounded, led by one of the brawniest of the factory boys, Bummer Pinnell he was called. I'd never seen a nastier piece of work.

Three of them grabbed me from behind.

'We'll settle with you in the Field,' Bummer said. 'Poor old Webby won't be up to footer this dinner-time after what you done to him.'

How Bummer knew who I was and where to come for me, I never knew: he worked in the stamping shop,

Webby was still in the frame shed and, only a few minutes had passed between the fight and the sounding of the dinner-time hooter. There was a kind of bush telegraph among the factory boys, and news could travel like wildfire through the shops and yards. The frame shed was almost guaranteed to be empty in the dinner hour. In some workshops – the rolling mills, the steam-hammer shop and the smith's shop – the eating of meals was allowed, but not in our shed. It was a safe bet that I would be there, because my grub had been stolen and I had no idea where else to go on my own. Country kids were no different, even when I left the Works. You could always tell the new ones: they stayed near their machines – it would be days before they would venture to the other end of the shop – and were rarely cheeky like town boys.

Bummer and his pals dragged me through the Works, past the new oil furnace and drop-stampers' forges, down long lines of wheel-bogies, great stone workshops and yards and past a hissing shunting engine to a scraggy waste they called the Field. There were about twenty lads there, all about my age or a little older, punting a football across the sooty grass; their jackets thrown down in piles for goal-posts. They stopped when they saw us coming.

'What you got there then, Bummer?'

'The new clodhopper. Him what went for Webby,' shouted Bummer.

'We'll give him a fight. He's a nasty little bugger – straight out the muckyard.'

They were all around me now, one poking me in the ribs. A greasy lout in a bulging tweed cap hacked me on my bruised ankle.

Then a shout went up.

'Give him to Snowball! Snowball will fix him.'

A tall lad stepped forward, stripping off his waistcoat and handed it to Bummer. I recognised him instantly. It was the fair-headed boy who had smacked me in the mouth in our fight at the rickyard in Liddiard Parva.

EIGHT

Snowball punched me in the mouth, just as he had done in the rickyard. I threshed about as best I could, but my heart wasn't in it. I can't scrap unless my blood is up. It was the same when I had to go in the ring in the training battalion. I was scared and I just didn't want to fight Snowball. It was soon over and I limped off back to the frame shed with a bruised mouth and a very painful shoulder.

It took me ages to find the way. I was shaken, and very hungry. And when I did get back, the chargehand started on at me about 'cow-bangers' and 'muck-spreaders' coming into the Works, keeping down the wages of honest townsmen.

The afternoon was worse than the morning. The din was louder than ever when the boilers were primed. The wheels whirled again and the shout went round to 'Hammer up'. I crept back to my place at the forge to jostle with the other rivet boys. The shed was even hotter than it was in the morning; the fumes from the machines mingled with those from the forge until I thought I would choke. The horseplay reduced me to a condition of numb despair. All this misery to produce the machines that we had toiled to catch a glimpse of on

Chick-Chack Day four years before. The *City of Truro* must have made her 100 mph run at about the time I went into the Works, but I was on the Carriage Side and I knew nothing and cared nothing about the great engines of Mr Dean and Mr Churchward. I tended the rivets in the blistering heat of the frame shed forge on my first day in the Works, and all I worried about was where the chargehand was and who was going to give me the next going-over or send me off on yet another useless errand to get my backside kicked.

I was squatting down behind one of the forges in the frame shed next morning, feeling very sorry for myself, when Snowball came and found me.

'Here, d'you want one of these?' he said, shoving a tattered book under my nose and crouching down beside me.

I took the book and nodded. I was too pleased and confused to know what to say.

'You didn't do so well yesterday as you done at Liddiard,' he said. 'It *was* you with that Ashbourne lot, all them years ago? When we had the scrap in old Peploe's rickyard?'

I nodded again, this time in real delight, but I was worried that Snowball would be fined half-a-crown – the penalty in the G.W.R. *Rules & Regulations* for a workman who went into a workshop in which he was 'not normally employed'. But Snowball didn't seem to care.

'How did you get back that day? We waited for ages and you never come?'

'We went on to Acorn Bridge. It was late when we come back. Jess's uncle was driving back with a waggon from Highworth and give us a ride. We hid behind some sacks when we come through Liddiard.'

'Why d'you go to Acorn Bridge?'

'It was daft, really – we wanted to see a railway engine.'

'Christ almighty, you'll see enough of they here,' Snowball said. 'Who was that girl with you – the big 'un, I mean?'

'Ruth. My sister.'

'She couldn't half scrap. Nearly killed old Sammy Fox with that bloody hayfork, her did.'

We chattered on as if we were two Crimean veterans remembering Balaclava. It was the first time I ever gossiped like that. We were quite good at it. I felt grown-up.

Snowball told me that his family had moved from Liddiard four years before just after the fight in the rickyard. His father had been bailiff at a large farm, but it had gone bankrupt: 'the one on the right afore you get to Acorn Bridge. You must have passed it after you left Liddiard when we had the fight, like.'

I nodded: I remembered the farm all right.

They had moved into town after that; they lived in a stone and slate cottage in one of the long terraced streets near the Works entrance. It had a proper lav built on at the back. His father hated the town; he was working as a shop clerk in the Locomotive Works, Snowball said.

I was going to say more, but our talk was sharply interrupted by the chargehand's bellow.

'Hey up, you young bugger – stop your magging and get on with it.'

I had no opportunity even to glance at Snowball's book until after the hooter sounded at dinner-time. In any case, my head was too full of thoughts about its giver, as I sweated away at the rivet forge.

The days were warm for October, so I ate my grub sitting by myself in the sunshine, shaded by a clump of weeds and leaning against a huge rusting boiler. When I had eaten – it didn't take long, I had only an onion and a lump of bread – I remembered Snowball's gift.

I fished it out of my pocket. On the disintegrating paper cover an extraordinary and rather feminine-looking man, with long hair falling on to his shoulders, was waving a smoking pistol.

I learned later that Snowball had been less than generous in giving me this penny dreadful in particular, for Buffalo Bill's popularity was in steep decline among the factory boys at that time. The craze was all for Deadwood Dick.

Snowball's book was called *The Tribunal of Ten, a Tale of Mystery and Love on the Rolling Prairie, Washington Territory* and I found it hard going. Not only because I had no practice – it had been all chanting of tables and being caned at Ashbourne School – but because of the spelling which, it took me some time to realise, had been deliberately distorted to represent American speech.

However, I soon mastered the idiom and started on an unremitting diet of Wild West tales. When I could not get Buffalo Bill or Deadwood Dick stories, I read Sexton Blake and sometimes comics such as *Union Jack* in the pink cover, and the *Marvel* or even the *Wonder*. But never the *Jester*: we all hated the *Jester*.

I was too tired to read when I got back to Ashbourne, especially in the darkness of autumn and winter evenings. I read mostly during the breakfast and dinner breaks in those first awful weeks in 13 Shop. As soon as I had thrown down my tools, I buried my head in one of those limp, tattered books, squatting beside a machine or a forge or, if it was not too cold, outside in the yard, where the air was less suffocating. My body was outside the frame shed, but my imagination was in South Dakota.

My reading habits infuriated some of the workmen.

'You'll addle your brain, filling it up with that muck.'

'Yankee rubbish! I reckon the bloke that wrote that stuff ought to be strung up hisself.'

Two of my most severe critics were Wormy Leach, a shambling labourer with close-set eyes – so-called for his habit of groping us rivet boys in the darker corners of the frame shed – and Mucky Bates, a cheerful Cockney with a drooping moustache and a pocketful of dirty postcards. These worried me more than Wormy's habits. They were of two kinds. The first depicted quite pretty ladies, in long flowing skirts and elaborate corsetry, being coyly disrobed by roughish men with twiddly moustaches and straw boaters. The second were of grotesquely sprawling, stark-naked women, with deathly white skins and horrible black hairs between their thighs. These upset and frightened me.

I pretended not to look at Mucky's pictures.

Calamity Jane was more to my taste – brave and dashing but chaste in riding breeches and check shirt, trying valiantly to retrieve the severed head of Deadwood Dick from the fairground showman who had pickled it in alcohol.

Surprisingly, the Gaffer seemed not to disapprove. He came twice to talk with me at breakfast-time in my first weeks in the frame shed and, on both occasions, he asked if he might see what I was reading.

'Well there's a thing – so that's the famous Deadwood Dick, is it?' He looked amused as he turned the pages, and his eyes twinkled. 'When I was a lad it was all Jack Harkaway: *Jack Harkaway's Schooldays*, there was, and *Jack Harkaway Among the Pirates*, I remember. What he didn't get up to wasn't worth doing, I can tell you.'

He was a good man, Mr Johnson, and so was Fred Stratton. I was his rivet boy for the best part of a year – and then his holder-up. Mr Stratton never swore at his mate, or at me if I let the metal drop, when he was rivetting; he would sometimes produce an acid drop or a humbug from a polished tin in his overall pocket, for me and the new rivet boy.

You get all sorts in the Works – like you do in a battalion – and just a very few of them are really fine men. I never met a better one than our Gaffer. And he ran an efficient shop, more or less, despite its unlucky number and the inevitable sprinkling of bad hats and twerps. Mr Johnson was a real buccaneer. He stoutly resisted any attempt to cut the prices for jobs. Once he stripped off his jacket, strode over to the forge and challenged some high-up of Churchward's staff whether he could do the job in quicker time. He could not bear any interference in his shop and yet he was not above conniving at the diversion of new machinery, intended for other workshops, to the frame shed. And he would expect us to back him up in his theft when he was in danger of being caught out.

'That drop-hammer's been here nigh on six weeks – ain't it, boy?' he'd say about a machine that had mysteriously appeared in the shop only the week before.

Like me, Mr Johnson was a voracious reader. Not in the Works, of course, but on Sundays and in the evenings, he told me, if he was not too tired after the day's work. His great favourite when I joined the frame shed was Walter Besant: '*Sir* Walter', as he would refer to him, with a mixture of deference and of pride – such as he might reserve for the skill of one of his own craftsmen.

'I shall have to get you on to *Sir* Walter,' he said to me once as he was examining some of Fred's frame rivetting, making Sir Walter sound more like a railway locomotive. 'We should get you on to *No Other Way*. It's about the abolition of slavery,' he explained with a twinkle in his eye and a wave of one of his huge hands.

But I had no intention of deserting Deadwood Dick, or Wild Bill Hickock: I was like an opium addict in a Sexton Blake mystery.

Snowball was in a penny dreadful syndicate and he got me into it. You could buy copies from several newsagents in the town and second-hand ones were regularly sold at the factory gates for next to nothing. If you got the right ones when it was your turn, then you could swap them with the other boys. Bummer Pinnell saw to it all. As Snowball spoke for me, Bummer let me join, although he was not keen on me playing football at dinner-time. But I had never played, so it didn't matter.

After my second week at the Works, Snowball took me home with him: after work on a cold, wet Saturday. There was no big football match in the town that afternoon – Snowball always went to those if he could. His father had gone to Wootton Bassett to see his sister, so there was only Snowball's mother and two of his sisters waiting for us when we turned from the end of a long alley of stone railway cottages and pushed open the green wooden gate into Snowball's backyard.

On the right of the tiny whitewashed enclosure, a green door stood ajar to reveal the gleaming white pan of the famous water closet. Ahead, the back door, also green, opened before Snowball's hand even touched the latch.

'You're late, Reginald.'

Snowball's mother was a busy, matronly little woman, long fair hair coiled about her ears. She hurried us through the steaming kitchen, which I noticed had been built-on, like the lardy cake woman's kitchen at Liddiard, and into the living-room. There was a freshly banked-up fire burning in the grate. Snowball's sisters, both younger than me – ten and eleven, maybe – were sitting waiting at the table. They both grinned shyly and fiddled with the cutlery.

Ivy and Ethel kept giggling, while Reginald – as his mother said I had to call Snowball – looked daggers at them. We had shepherd's pie and boiled cabbage and then suet pudding with treacle on top. I remember glancing furtively around the room: it was so grand, with a peg rug on a slippery oil-cloth floor, a black marble clock, Staffordshire figures on the bobble-fringed mantelshelf, and shining brass gas lamps. Even the names Reginald and Ethel and Ivy were ravishingly modern. They made the Thursas, Ruths and Absolems of Ashbourne seem dowdy and shameful.

There was unimaginable luxury in the front parlour: a polished sideboard covered in knick-knacks, pictures on every wall (some in golden frames), a huge aspidistra in a large fawn-coloured pot, decorated with a pattern of roses, standing near a net-curtained window on a deli-cate mahogany stand. Above the fireplace was a large sepia photograph of an imposing, whiskered man in a stiff collar gazing wistfully across the crowded, glit-tering furniture.

There was no fire in the front parlour, but after dinner I was content to sit on the sofa with Snowball as the rain fell outside, happily swinging my legs, until his mother asked me to stop it. I was not altogether sure that she approved of me. She was very polite; she seemed the sort who could never have been anything else. But I sensed that I did not fit in. I later discovered that I was right, both about me and about her. Snowball's mother was a foreman's daughter who had married a young farm bailiff she met at a picnic outing to Bourton. His father had owned his own farm and lost it just as Snow-ball's father had with the farm at Liddiard Parva. She had never liked the country and preferred to live in splendour on the princely twenty-five shillings wage of a workshop clerk.

Snowball told me, as we sat side by side on the sofa, that he had an elder sister who had gone with her father, straight from work, to Wootton Bassett; Mabel worked in a nearby garment factory, and her mother did not like it. And then I rabbited on about the downs behind the village and Wayland Smith's cave and milking machines and ferreting. But it all seemed far away and unimportant in the gleaming reality of Snowball's front parlour. I noticed his slight stutter and the way the corners of his mouth creased when he grinned at me.

I had to tramp all the way back to Ashbourne later that wet afternoon; I did not go through Liddiard, but along the big road that skirted the northern face of the downs. It was dusk when I slithered up the chalk track to the cottage amid the wailing calls of stone curlews and the smell of pigs.

NINE

In the Works I was always a yokel. One of the clod-hoppers who appeared mysteriously at the factory gates to threaten the livelihood of honest railwaymen. Never a day passed in my whole time in 13 Shop when this was not rubbed in, good-humouredly or in malice. As country lads have before, and I expect always will in the factory at least, I kept my head down and got on with the work — and consoled myself with penny dreadfuls.

Things were different in Ashbourne. There I had acquired an unexpected lustre as I roamed the fields with Tiger, Pebbie and Jess on Sunday afternoons or swanked with Stiffy and Bodger as we strode back on Saturdays with factory grime deliberately left on our hands and faces.

Tales of mighty steam engines, the ways of the great town and the depravity of factory life became my stock-in-trade, embellished often with episodes that had more to do with Deadwood Dick or Sexton Blake than with Isambard Kingdom Brunel's Great Western Railway Company. The wonders of the new electric tramway lost nothing in the telling. The blood-curdling account I gave of the murder of poor Hettie Swinford at the Ship Hotel would have done credit to the man who wrote

Sweeney Todd. And such was the vividness of my descriptions of the female anatomy depicted in Mucky's postcards that Jess refused to speak to his mother for a week. Not that I had everything my own way in Ashbourne. There was always the treadmill of farm work, and though I now thought myself an urban sophisticate, I had to do my turn in the fields when Mr Thorne decreed it or if my father ordered me on to our own little patch.

Such time as I could get to myself, I spent mooching around Ashbourne, often with Pebbie or Jess or Tiger – occasionally with all three – in pursuit of the wildlife of the downland or watercress beds. Tiger had stolen some snares and a gin trap from his father and great was our satisfaction when we heard the agonised squeals of a captive hare on misty Sunday mornings.

I was now deeply ashamed of Ashbourne and the downland and its backward country ways, but deeper still I was drawn back to it. Indeed, there was nowhere else I could have gone for I was an outsider in the town, and always would be.

Tiger particularly was excited by my boasting about the G.W.R. and the Works in which I was such an insignificant cog. He had little trouble in persuading his father that he too should be allowed to try his luck at the factory gates.

I spoke to Fred Stratton about Tiger coming into the frame shed, Fred put in a good word with the Gaffer and Mr Johnson agreed to inspect John Clack's pal from Ashbourne. He took one look and, within the hour, Tiger was in the iron foundry.

'Sorry, young'un,' the Gaffer growled, 'but your friend is temperamentally suited to molten metal and red hot ashes. He's going to turn out a right little heller, I reckon.'

Jess and Pebbie followed Tiger into the Works in the spring of 1905. They stayed together in the wheel shop. It was a curious choice for Pebbie Titcombe; it was the cleanest shop in the Works, with no furnaces or forges to belch out muck. They both went straight on to the lathes and seemed to do very well from the very beginning. Not that I saw much of them in the factory, but we used to lark about on the cart on the way back to Ashbourne, much to the Liddiard men's irritation. We would walk out of Liddiard Parva in a tight formation, with Stiffy and Bodger, and a couple of other Ashbourne lads who had started in the carriage body shop at about the same time as Tiger went into the iron foundry. But there was never any real trouble with the Liddiard lads like that scrap in the rickyard five years before.

The money we brought into the village was a godsend. Ten years ago I must have been bringing home more than Mr Thorne paid my father, even allowing for the money I paid as my share of the waggon from Liddiard Parva. But for some of the old'uns it was the beginning of the end for Ashbourne. The men went on endlessly about the passing of the good old days. About the club anniversary, when Jimmy Bunce used to carry the huge, red-tasselled flag, with the band playing and how there was a sit-down meal of roast beef, before the money was paid out. How old Jemmy Kemble could push a breast-plough better than anyone this side of Sevenhampton. About motor cars and these new-fangled milking machines which would debilitate honest cows. The women were worse, if anything. It was always the same with them, from Granny Bowles to Mrs Storey-Ellis: continual lamentations about the flighty ways of the village girls and what their old grandmothers would have said about them and how Mrs Thorne couldn't get anyone to scrub the farmhouse floors because they were getting so uppity – buying *shop* dresses and all – and going off into service, leaving only girls like Thursa Simcock – and she was daft in the head and no better than she ought to be.

I heard them at it in the lane as I sprawled behind our hedge on a drowsy July afternoon with a handful of gooseberries and the bees humming overhead. It was the day after Ruth had left to go into service at Lambourne and I was a bit fed-up. I was immersed in Sexton Blake's life and death struggle with the Brotherhood of the Yellow Beetle. It was the Monday of Trip Week, '05. I was fourteen, recently promoted to holder-up, and glorying in the seven days of freedom from No. 13 Shop on the Works annual holiday. Fred Stratton and his mates had been almost skittish on the Friday before; for weeks, apprentices had ticked off the days on a makeshift calendar they had chalked on the workshop wall.

Snowball had gone off to Weymouth with his family. They always went there, he said, and had left early on Saturday morning in one of the dozens of special Trip trains. Snowball said half the town would be leaving – about twenty-five thousand according to Mr Stratton, who was off to Weston-super-Mare; they had to load up in the Works sidings, with special steps to climb up to the coaches. According to Snowball, one of the Weymouth trains would be hauled by the *City of Truro*, but I suspected that that was wishful thinking.

I was not particularly bothered about staying at home. None of the Ashbourne lads went anywhere. It would have been inconceivable for our families to have gone to the seaside – even for only the day, as many of the townspeople did – and, in any case, none of us had paid our shillings to join the Mechanics' Institute, which was necessary to get free travel.

Tiger came up the lane for me later that afternoon. He was nonchalant in an unbuttoned waistcoat and clean white shirt, open at the neck: a costume by which we factory boys signalled to the village that we were at leisure. It was much too early for harvest, so we had a bit of time to ourselves on Trip Week in Ashbourne, although it infuriated my father, especially if he found me with my head in a book.

We climbed on to the downs, as we had five years before on Chick-Chack Day; skylarks overhead, and the great sweep of the Vale of the White Horse behind us. They say you can see seven counties from Ashbourne Down, but heat haze dimmed the horizon and I could barely make out the tiny billow of steam moving steadily westward beyond Liddiard Parva. I thought with envy of Snowball at the seaside in Weymouth.

At the summit we flung ourselves down on the sward, gazing up at a solitary cumulus, towering like a white fist against the sky.

Tiger told me that he had fought with his father that morning: there had been a row about feeding the whippet. I could never really be Snowball's friend, he said. He was far too popular for the likes of me. Later that evening we snared two rabbits. We heard them screaming behind the thorns at the top of the chalk track as we walked down the coombe.

I must have been seventeen before I went on a Trip Week excursion. It was the year we turned out *The Great Bear*: 142 tons, with fifteen-inch cylinders – the first Pacific locomotive to have been made in England. We were as proud of her on the Carriage Side as if we had built her ourselves. I slipped out to watch her steam out of A Shop on a raw February morning.

It was a worrying time in the Works. A lot of men were laid off and when that happened the country blokes who were kept on got it in the neck for stealing the jobs of honest townsmen. Fortunately, none of the Ashbourne crew were sacked that year or we wouldn't have been on the excursion to Weston-super-Mare.

We set off from the village at four o'clock in the morning. We had to walk all the way, but there was a fine dawn and we took the road along the edge of the downs which I always preferred.

We were three fine fellows – Jess, Tiger and me – striding along the winding flint road from Ashbourne, caps on the back of our heads, with not a motor car or waggon in sight in the clear light of a July morning.

The sidings were packed when we got to the Works – jostling women in wide hats and excited children with buckets and spades; the men resplendent in dark Sunday suits, some with straw hats, most carrying hampers or bags – all jammed next to the huge wheels of rows of steaming locomotives and the long lines of carriages, with wooden steps to climb aboard. The noise and excitement in the crowded carriages was intense. We all cheered as the train began to move and we lurched slowly across the points and intersecting rails with a whoop of the engine whistle.

Those were glorious moments when we steamed away from the factory sidings and the grey stone workshops. You forgot the long months of labour and the grumbling; the grime and din of 13 Shop. The *County of Monmouth* – long and green and gleaming with brass – was hauling us westward to the sea.

We arrived in a whirl of excitement and headed straight for the Marine Parade. It was signposted, so we knew which way to go.

The tide was far out, the sea a brown smudge across

acres of pungent mud. Everything was brisk and maritime in the bright sunshine under a huge sky: union jacks cracked in the breeze; donkeys hauled small children across the immense sands in graceful little four-wheeled waggons; the Grand Pier rose high above us, blindingly white and new, on spindly seaweedy legs. We stood gawping up in its shadow.

It was all so different from the lonely headlands, the tropic beaches and the rocky northern shores that sometimes adorned the covers of Chatto & Windus's 'sixpenny wonderfuls', as the Gaffer called them. At seventeen, I was as green as grass: I had actually imagined that the rows of prim seaside boarding-houses – which I knew about from Snowball and Fred Stratton – would give way to soaring cliffs and a foaming sea – or to a lonely bay with weedy rocks like the one on which Franklin Blake stood in *The Moonstone*, hauling up poor Rosanna Spearman's japanned tin case from the Shivering Sand by its rusty iron chain.

But the busy beach at Weston-super-Mare was not at all like that, except for the mud which could engulf the unwary almost as effectively as the quicksands at Cobb's Hole that Wilkie Collins described.

We sat at the top of the beach, trying to rub the stuff off our boots with handfuls of damp sand. It was humiliating, that floundering about on the mud flats, looking for the ocean. Things were not helped when a gaggle of skinny girls of about our age – all in broad-brimmed straw hats and calf-length white skirts – shrieked at us in uncouth northern tones.

'You can bugger off and all,' Tiger shouted, scrubbing away at his miry turn-ups. Jess threw a pebble with a satisfying thump against the ribs of a passing spaniel.

'Wonder what old Pebbie's doing?' Tiger growled, as the dog chi-iked and a passing army sergeant gave Jess a funny look. It was Tiger's idea: Pebbie would have mucked things up – and he still smelled like a midden.

'He'll know we've been here,' said Jess.

'We'll get him a stick of rock and some winkles for his ferret,' Tiger said and laughed.

We wandered along the Marine Parade, in the brilliant sunlight, weaving through the dark-clad crowds of strolling trippers, the brisk sea smells still sharp in our nostrils. We spotted Mucky Bates wearing a straw boater, with his rat-faced wife at his side, and a couple of Jess's mates from the wheel shop, one of them with a girl on his arm. She was laughing up into his face, clutching the brim of her hat as she did so.

It was some more of Jess's factory pals who got us into The Cooper's Arms. They were standing outside, eating pasties from paper bags, with pink earthenware mugs in their fists, and their caps pushed back on their heads.

'Look what the tide have washed up,' one of them called across the street in his sing-song townee voice.

'Still got muck on their boots by the look of 'em.'

I thought Tiger was going to go for him, but Jess stepped in and everything was all right.

'Going to buy us a drink, Chucky?'

'Might do – if you buy us one first.'

'All right then,' said Jess. 'What'll it be?'

And that's how we started the pub crawl at Weston-super-Mare. I am sure that none of us really enjoyed it. But it seemed the right thing for six young railway men beside the western sea – even if we couldn't actually find it.

We drank rough cider: Chucky said it was stronger than beer. It was certainly cheaper. The Weston land-lords bought it in from local farmers who sold it for twopence a pint; according to a cross-eyed drayman we met in the public bar, they coloured it with blood.

From The Cooper's Arms we moved to The London, and then to The Swan and on to The Plough.

I sipped cautiously at the raw, yellow fluid. But this only delayed the inevitable. My head stayed clear enough, but I could hardly make it to The Plough. My legs seemed to be working independently, and Jess kept jostling me. He had become uncharacteristically ill-tempered, and kept lurching into me.

It was unbearably hot. In the Winter Gardens, we encountered the white-skirted trollops, now in line abreast; arms linked, a fat one in the middle, her bonnet awry. Their shrieks drowned the faint rhythmic thumpings of a brass band and pierced my brain like steel needles.

I felt sick, and extremely tired, and dared not stop in case I fell over. So I tottered on between neat rectangular beds of scarlet tea roses and sedate strolling couples, leaving the others to swap insults with the northern trollops.

Eventually, I found myself back on the Marine Parade after nearly walking under a tram-car and falling down on the Winter Garden steps. I got some very dirty looks. The beach was packed. I weaved my way between deck-chairs and donkeys and sandcastles and picnics; it seemed more like Highworth Fair, with striped canvas stalls and a Punch and Judy show. There was still no sign of the ocean, only an immensity of mud and, beyond it, the grey smudge of Steepholme island.

I stopped at the seaward edge of the crowd, and slumped down on the damp compacted sand, shut my eyes and dreamed of Snowball at Weymouth.

It was odd, that cider-sodden dream. I can still remember bits of it. Weymouth was circled with hills, taller than Ashbourne Down. Streets ran steeply down to a blue sea, lapping the harbour steps at the end of a wide bay enclosed by rocky headlands. We lived in a thatched, white-washed cottage at the foot of precipitous cliffs with a secret zig-zag path among the woods at the top. Our beach was in a narrow cove, alive with sea bird calls. Drawn up on the pebbles was a sturdy rowing boat, white with a dark blue gunwale.

Snowball and I spent much of our time fishing and exploring the rock pools. Our stay at the cottage was blissfully happy, until the boat sank and Snowball drowned at my side. As the sea water crept up my body, Christ came across the water towards me, arms outstretched, and the hem of his white robe floating. He bent forward − and spoke in Tiger's voice.

'What the bloody hell are you doing here?'

I opened my eyes and found the Bristol Channel lapping my waist.

'We been looking for you all afternoon, you silly bugger.'

Tiger was cross.

'Buggered everything up you have. Chucky reckons they're going to shag they Brummy girls.'

I sat next to Mucky Bates on the journey home. My trousers were still soaking and my head ached. Tiger and Jess slept as soon as we pulled out of the Locking Road excursion platform. Mrs Bates nodded off before we passed Yatton, her mouth open, her straw hat clamped vertically against the upholstery.

Mucky was depressed. He too had been drinking and seemed strangely vulnerable without his postcards.

'It'll be the grand march past again, Friday next,' he grumbled. 'Straight past the pay table and not a brass farthing to last out the week.'

He paused and gazed mournfully out at the flat Somerset fields and the distant escarpment of the Mendips, bluey-grey in the late afternoon sunlight.

'That's the next thing old Jimmy Thomas'll have to get the Associated Society of poor bloody Railway Servants to sort out now he's a big pot in London.'

Mucky glared across the compartment at his crumpled wife and fished out a packet of Woodbines.

'You didn't know old Jimmy, I suppose. Funny little bloke, had lopsided ears. On the footplate he was – a pilotman. Used to bring in the morning shift from Wootton Bassett most days, he did. He put the wind up Mr high-and-mighty Stanier. Locomotive Manager or no, Jimmy kicked him out of Queen's Ward in the last elections and he called our union meetings in the Mechanics' Institute. Old Churchward didn't want them on GWR property, but there was nothing he could do about it, what with Jimmy being a town councillor and all.'

Mucky put his hand on my knee and then thought better of it.

'But you bumpkins don't have nothing to do with the union. More worried about your swedes than anything else.'

Mucky went on and on about Jimmy Thomas and Reuben George and socialism – and the blacklegging by clodhoppers and muckspreaders. He was right about us Ashbourne lads: we were just glad of the money and my gaffer was a saint compared with Mr Thorne or Mrs Storey-Ellis if it came to that.

I dozed, while Mucky droned away in my ear, and dreamed fitfully of sea birds calling on a sunlit shore.

There was a juddering of brakes. The familiar factory buildings slid by: the long grey outline of the iron foundry and the serried windows of the erecting shop.

Other excursion trains were steaming back into the sidings in the evening light. One after another they came in: *County of Somerset*, *Lady of Quality*, *Saint Ambrose* –

107

hauling long caterpillars of chocolate and cream carriages, tired pale faces at every window.

The next one to ours had just run in from Weymouth. A town lad of about my age, from A Shop, was clambering down the wooden steps as I walked in the shadows between the lines of carriages with Tiger and Jess. He called after us and then said that Snowball had been taken ill at Weymouth and was in hospital. Snowball had gone swimming that afternoon and had collapsed when he came out of the sea.

TEN

They brought Snowball back on the last excursion train from Weymouth. They wheeled his coffin from the guard's van on a factory barrow, and then on the shoulders of some returning A Shop men, to rest beneath his grandfather's frozen stare in the cluttered parlour of the cottage near the Works entrance.

Snowball had had meningitis: it flared up almost as soon as he arrived at Weymouth. He was dead before Trip Week was over.

They buried him in the family grave at Liddiard Parva. The Gaffer gave me the day off to go to the funeral. I was the only one from Ashbourne who went.

The tenor bell tolled as I passed the lardy cake woman's house. She was standing at her gate: a dark figure in a black dress, hair drawn tight into the same white bun at the nape of her neck. It was the first time I had seen her since the fight in the rickyard with Snowball, even though I had walked that way every working day for years.

The bell echoed across the flat countryside, the intervals so long that each seemed as if it must be the last. It was hot that morning. The heat seeped through the shoulders of my jacket; my cap band was damp with sweat.

Swifts were skimming and squealing among the gravestones, as I turned through the lych gate into Liddiard churchyard. There was a bulky, surpliced figure standing at the door. Not the daft one who had cornered us there all those years before: this one was older and darker and fatter – and obviously bored – with piggy eyes and gold-rimmed spectacles. He nodded brusquely as I passed.

The coffin was in the side chapel where the old woman's body had lain. Snowball's mother was at the back of the church, standing with Ivy and Ethel and their father. They were all in black, their faces puffy and strangely distorted. There was another girl with them, leaning against a pillar: Mabel, I supposed. Her hair was fair like Snowball's, and fell on to her shoulders, but that was all I could see for her face was turned away.

Some of Snowball's mates from A shop were in the Lady Chapel. One was Bummer Pinnell. Another was the barrel-chested lad who stole my red handkerchief on the day I fought Snowball in the Works. Awkward, like dummies, in their dark Sunday suits, they stood – caps folded under their arms – in the coloured light from the stained glass. The Virgin gazed down at her plaster babe; the smell of polish and flowers was overpowering.

I crouched in an empty pew at the back of the nave. The bell tolled again. Then the silence grew, broken only by occasional shufflings and the faint squealing of swifts. After what seemed an age, came the measured tread of feet and a man's voice – unctuous, yet matter-of-fact and unconcerned – echoing up to the decorated hammer-beam roof.

'I am the resurrection and the life . . . and though after my skin worms destroy this body, yet in my flesh shall I see God . . . we brought nothing into this world, and it is certain we carry nothing out . . .'

God knows, I've seen enough burials since I have been in Flanders. Yet I still remember Snowball's all right. Not that there was much to recall, really. Just the varnished planks of the pew floor and a faded purple hassock, embroidered with fleurs-de-lis and the voice – that damned voice – and the heat – and my own bloody misery.

There were some village kids in the churchyard when we came out. They pushed by me, near the church door. One of them shouted as they chased away, 'Over here, they're going to put him down the hole.'

I did not go into the Works that day, nor ride back on the waggons with some of the others for drinks and a bait at Snowball's house. After the service, I just plodded back to Ashbourne in the heavy July heat, slurped some water from the pump by Granny Bailey's cottage and headed for the chalk track on to the downs, as I had with Tiger and Jess and Pebbie on the day I fought Snowball at Liddiard Parva.

The Reverend-high-and-mighty-Gould spotted me by Thorne's rickyard as he came riding down from the coombe.

He reined in his grey gelding. Lifting his panama and mopping his brow, he glared down at me with cold, narrow eyes.

'What are you doing about the village at this time of day, Clack? Thought the Railway Works closed *last* week.'

Somehow, I managed the required idiot grin, mumbling about a funeral.

'That was for Billy Horton's boy, wasn't it? The one who was bailiff at Liddiard?'

I nodded.

'Friend of yours was he?'

I nodded again, near to tears and rebellion.

'Unlucky family that. Horton let the farm go shame-fully.'

And that was that as far as the twenty-ninth Vicar of Ashbourne was concerned. He rode on, swiping at circling flies with his panama.

There had not been a breath of air in the valley and on Ashbourne Down the breeze scarcely caused a tremor among the wayside bents. The whole rolling landscape was weighed down under the heat with the distant ridges of the downs hidden in dull haze. Even the crows seemed too listless to squabble over the bones of a dead sheep. There were no bird sounds, only the bees buzzing through the hot air. Away to the south, a column of smoke rose and merged with the haze.

I started along the green road, heading east along the chalk escarpment towards Uffington Camp. I had no idea why I was going that way. But in the village they say you can walk on the Ridgeway from one side of the country to the other. And everywhere, strung out along its way, are the handiworks of the old people, all dead and gone: their barrows, earthwork camps, terraced fields and standing stones – left to the skylarks and sheep and Sluggie Bunce in his tall wooden caravan. An empty landscape that chimed with my desolation.

I barely managed a mile before I seized up and flung myself down in a hawthorn's shade.

I lay there, cap pulled over my face, thinking of the poor devils sweating at the forges in 13 Shop and of my mother, hot and tired, scrubbing away at the dairy floor, far below among the farmyard elms – and of Snowball cool in his grave beneath the valley haze.

It had not been much of a thing my friendship with Snowball: just a couple of fights, a few jaunts on Saturday afternoons, some borrowed penny dreadfuls and a lot of imagination about the companion I would have liked him to have been. It was the only choice I had ever tried to make for myself. Everything else in life had been issued to me, like a recruit his equipment at Roundway Barracks. Perhaps that is why it hurt so much. And the feeling of being alone, trapped without choice: left to help bang in rivets and touch my cap to the Reverend Gould and go ferreting with Tiger and Pebbie Titcombe on Sunday mornings.

I was back in the frame shed the next morning. No one mentioned Snowball – or his funeral. Not even Fred Stratton. I suppose there was no reason why any of the others should have known of my one-sided friendship with a lad from the Locomotive Side or have the energy to bother about it in the awful heat, which built up to a fair imitation of hell after breakfast that day.

The rivet boys suffered terribly from working so close to the forges. Some of them wrapped wet cleaning rags round their heads and they all gulped down water by the bucketful in the meal-breaks and whenever the chargehand's back was turned. The Gaffer wangled some oatmeal from the stores which we mixed with the water at dinner-time, to make it more palatable and, according to the Gaffer, to offset the harmful effects of drinking such vast quantities of the factory article. My head ached and my shirt was soaking with perspiration. Dust and fumes hung, shimmering in blinding shafts of sunlight. Half-choked and exploding with heat, it was as much as I could do to hold up for Fred Stratton with weary arms and an aching back.

We swam in the mill pool that evening, Tiger, Pebbie, Jess and me. Not that we had planned to. As we straggled back into the village, we just kicked off our boots, flung down our clothes and leapt in – bollock-naked.

Thursa Simcock watched us from the bridge. She ran off when Tiger chased her, but was back as soon as he jumped in again.

The weather broke that night. Great mountains of clouds piled up to the south-west at dusk and, as darkness fell, a cool wind blew across the downs from Hackpen way, scattering the loose straw in Thorne's rickyard and lashing a branch of our pear tree against the cottage dormer. The thunder echoed and rumbled among the dark hills well into the night before the storm struck in full force with sheet lightning and torrential rain that poured from our thatch like a waterfall, as I lay in a fitful dream of Snowball drowning in the cove at Weymouth.

The morning dawned fresh and bright, with a cool breeze ruffling the battered wild flowers as we marched to work. Tiger was still excited at the violence of the storm and by his naked pursuit of Thursa Simcock from the mill pool. He said that Aaron Spiller had got drunk the night before, then fallen asleep in a ditch bottom and been half drowned in a torrent of water when the storm broke.

The Gaffer was waiting for me at the door of the frame shed. He had come in early that morning and was standing watching a pair of factory rooks tearing away at a lump of bread that some poor devil must have chucked away in the heat of the day before.

The Gaffer looked up and took the pipe from his mouth.

'Sorry to hear about your pal going so sudden like that,' he said. 'Fred Stratton told me about it, but what with the goings-on in the shed yesterday, I didn't get round to talking to you about it.'

He thrust a hand into his jacket pocket and shifted uneasily.

'I lost a pal once when I was about your age. In Dorset it was,' the Gaffer continued, staring down at his gleaming boots and pushing his bowler to the back of his head in embarrassment. 'Hung himself he did. It was a queer go, right enough. Dressed in his sister's clothes he was. They'd hung a woman that day for killing her kids and my mate . . . did what he did . . . sort of *reenacted* it, like.'

The Gaffer gazed intently at the rooks as they hopped away behind an iron bogey.

'Not that there was anything funny about your pal though. He had a clean end.'

What in hell was this all about?

'It helps to read a good book when you're upset like,' the Gaffer went on, pulling a volume from his pocket. 'And a bit of music helps. It did when I lost my little girl. She had meningitis and all. I liked to go to a concert at The Mechanics then, especially when it was the G.W.R. Band and they played something good, like "The Rosary" by Ethelbert Nevin. That still brings tears to my eyes, I can tell you. But I feels wonderfully better after.'

The Gaffer glanced round furtively and held out the book for me.

'Here put this away now — and get on with your work. Mustn't let anything get in the way of that.'

I still have the secondhand sixpenny wonderful which the Gaffer shoved into my hand that morning. The cover is most extraordinary. Stomping along through a rocky desert landscape is a very grumpy-looking and extremely ancient Red Indian squaw. Bent over — like a decrepit version of Mr Gladstone — she is towing, by the hand, an idiotic looking cowboy in a floppy stetson hat that would have rested more appropriately on the head of a seventeenth-century dandy.

The Golden Butterfly combined the Gaffer's passion for *Sir* Walter with what, he imagined, was still my obsession with the Wild West. But I had deserted Deadwood Dick and all of his ilk years before, and was none too keen on Walter Besant, if it comes to that. Yet I am more grateful than I can ever say to the Gaffer for his kindness to me then.

It was the Gaffer who pushed me into joining the Mechanics' Institute and I thank him for that as well. He got Fred Stratton to take me there after work one Saturday to enrol and pay my sub. The Gaffer was all for self-improvement: lectures on electromagnetism and paper-making and the like. But I made straight for the Mechanics' Library. I had never seen anything like it before – or since, for that matter. On Saturday afternoons, and sometimes in my dinner-hour in the week, I would creep about on the gleaming floor, between the tall mahogany shelves – as proud as any scholar at Oxford University – trying to stop my boots squeaking, glorying in the leathery smell of the thousands upon thousands of volumes, each one specially bound and stamped in gold at the foot of the spine, 'G.W.R. Mechanics' Institution'.

I hit on the stratagem of hunting among the rows of returned books, by the librarian's desk. There were some heady hauls: Gustave Flaubert, G. A. Henty and Arnold Bennett; Henley, Stevenson, Kipling – and the author of *She* and *King Solomon's Mines* and *Ayesha*.

Sir Henry Rider Haggard became, for me, what *Sir* Walter was for the Gaffer, and Allan Quartermain as compelling as Deadwood Dick had been when I squatted outside the frame shed in the late autumn sun with the tattered penny dreadful that Snowball gave me.

I can still remember the exact moment when I opened *King Solomon's Mines*. It was a close Saturday afternoon, following a damp morning. I had stopped at a field gate to cool down and to gawp at some woodpigeons. They usually start feeding on ripening wheat at that time in August. There were the monotonous repetitions of yellowhammers, a suggestion of thunder across the downs; thistledown floated in the still air.

Leaning against the five-barred gate that humid afternoon, I slid into the adventures of Allan Quartermain and his pals: the quest for Sir Henry Curtis's brother and the hunt for Solomon's mines, their first encounter with Twala − the one-eyed king − and his terrifying hag, Gagool.

I finished the novel that night, sitting at the open dormer under the thatch, with moths spiralling and singeing around the candle flame and the smell of pigs floating in from the darkness.

So many things drew me to Haggard's Africa: open space and huge skies − I imagined like the Marlborough Downs, only hotter and larger − and the specialness of being English in that blood-stained continent. Like me − as I saw myself, at least − Quartermain was alone, wife and son dead, thrown among companions to do as he chose: as I had been with Tiger and Jess at Weston. Underlying everything was the empire, mightier even than the G.W.R.

They were kids' books, I suppose. But they were what I wanted in the aftermath of Snowball's death. Straightforward, old-fashioned bust-ups in foreign parts: preferably Africa, with Zulu impis, a mysterious native queen and some German or Portuguese bastards to kick the hell out of towards the end.

A few of the older men in the Works had been in the South African War. There was a man called Cottrell in the frame shed. He came from up north somewhere, and had been at Mafeking. And there was a smith, Tommy Bouchier – ex-hussar – a morose giant of a man with mutton-chop whiskers, a wounded leg and bad breath who had been at Spion Kop and, afterwards, rode into Ladysmith with Sir Redvers Buller.

I loved their yarns, although I was about the only one in the mess room who did. At breakfast-time I would sit behind them, choking in the tobacco smoke, waiting for talk of kaffirs and kopjes, armoured trains and commandos.

My head was full of such things: dreams of glory in foreign lands – that bore remarkable resemblance to the Vale of the White Horse – all enflamed by Haggard's fertile imaginings. It was pure adventure I was after. I suppose that was why youngsters donned scarlet tunics to blow the guts out of each other with muskets at point-blank range – or why so many of them are lying in khaki in the Flanders' mud.

ELEVEN

One sunny October afternoon, when everyone else seemed to be at the town football match, I came across a familiar name in the Mechanics' Library. It was on the spine of a book by the Gaffer's idol: 'A Eulogy of Richard Jefferies', it said – in crisp gold letters – by *Sir* Walter Besant.

This Jefferies, it turned out, was a writer – although as mad as a hatter, according to the Gaffer, who had never read a word that he had written. What is more, Mr Jefferies had been *local*: born at Coate, but dead and gone these twenty years, the Gaffer said. And *Bevis* was proof of it. It was another kids' book, but good enough for me.

That Sunday, I walked over to Coate and then right round the Long Pond – glittering in late summer sunshine – where Jefferies's youthful characters, Bevis and Mark, launched their cohorts against Ted Pompey and Scipio Cecil in their recreation of the Battle of Pharsalia. The Council Oak was exactly as Jefferies had described it, with its leaning hollow trunk in whose shade Bevis and Mark had argued and raged with Ted and the other village boys – Phil and 'Charl' and Val and Bob – about the lines of battle and the rules of war. And there was the

Straits of Mozambique, where the Long Pond narrowed, opposite the crumbling quarry where Caesar Bevis fell and was rescued in the great storm by Mark in the leaking punt in the aftermath of battle.

The Amateur Poacher, the next of Jefferies's books that I came across, was another revelation. I had been mooching around the hedgerows and coombes and watercress beds with Pebbie and Tiger and Jess since ever I could remember, wreaking mayhem among the wildlife. But I had no idea of the true art of the poacher. How you could make a 'squailer': a length of ground ash sapling with a heavy knob at one end, made by dipping it in a tea cup used as a mould for molten lead. If thrown right, it would fly as straight as a bullet to knock over a leveret or fetch out a squirrel from a tree. How you should use a circular noose to catch a jack, an oval one for a trout; thin double wires are better than single ones and copper superior to brass which is not so flexible and too conspicuous in the water. It was all there. How to find pheasant eggs or net partridges on September nights. Mr Jefferies knew about ferreting as well. It had never occurred to me that you could get a woodcock, or even a wild duck, with a fine horse-hair noose laid flat on the ground, attached to a pliant stick bent into the earth.

If he knows what he is about, a country poacher can have more skills than the smartest fitter and turner on the Locomotive Side. I drew much comfort from the thought. No longer would I be the frame-shed yokel, but a skilled and cunning hunter. And there would be adventure – and danger: a Wiltshire Allan Quartermain.

But there would be slim chance of this in Ashbourne. There were no gamekeepers, not even a warrener, in the village and only the occasional farmer's shoots; Father was allowed to take rabbits and – skinflint though he was – Old Thorne turned a blind eye when we scythed a sitting partridge in the harvest corn. If I should be discovered snaring a pheasant – and they were pretty scarce in Ashbourne – the worst I would get would be a kick in the backside and made to look like a damned fool, which would not have happened to Sir Henry Curtis and his lot.

Liddiard Parva was altogether a better prospect, with the Wynyard estate and keepers galore. What is more, I knew my way around Liddiard and the locals were used to Ashbourne lads passing through.

Tiger was the obvious ally.

I broached the idea when we were sitting on the mill bridge.

'Us'll need nets. And whatever else this bloke Jefferies used,' Tiger pondered, pitching a flint at a passing coot. 'Sounds a clever bugger he do.'

Tiger reckoned that he could make squailers in the iron foundry and we pulled up ground ash saplings there and then, hacking off fifteen-inch lengths for the shafts.

We practised with them on Ashbourne Down the following Saturday afternoon. With their heavy lead knobs and pliant shafts they were surprisingly accurate and – as often as not – could decapitate a dead thistle at twenty yards.

Our first success was a stone curlew, 'thick knees' as they were called in the village. We got it at dusk as it tried to creep into gathering gloom with slow, cautious strides of its long, knobbly legs. Later, I winged a moorhen by the feeder stream and got wet boots chasing it – flapping and splashing – among the watercress.

That was about all we got for a couple of weeks: squailers were not, it turned out, that easy to use.

By my enthusiasm for Mr Jefferies was undiminished. It was not just poaching. Every hedgerow, wild flower, farm gate and creeping insect took on new meaning. I tripped the light fantastic through meadows that I had plodded across since childhood; the familiar grey-green downs became a shimmering backdrop in late October sunlight; the chink-chink calling of chaffinches was silvery in the early morning air.

Richard Jefferies of Coate Farm gave me a sense of place and of belonging – with a kind of dignity, I suppose – and there had not been much of that for an uneducated Ashbourne bumpkin from the frame shop without a farthing to spare to scratch his backside at the end of the week.

I still handed my wage-packet to Mother. We were living better by then (at least we were not half-starved), but our decaying thatch leaked – and stank – and there were the same old sacks covering the crumbling brick floors. And Mother still worked in the fields and scrubbed out the Thorne's dairy every day, and curtsied to Mr Gould, when he rode past in the lane without so much as a lift of his riding-crop.

Looking back, I am surprised that Tiger should have been so cautious about poaching: he reckoned that it would take months for us to come up to scratch if we were going to do it properly. But then I have never been able to fathom him.

And it was Tiger who soon threw caution to the wind by launching our first real poaching foray at Kington Winlow: it all started at the public in Liddiard. It had changed a good deal since 1900, when we had marched through the village on Chick-Chack Day, but was still filthy and as different as could be from the Carpenter's Arms, or the Shepherd's Rest across the downs, where the floors were scrubbed and the worst that happened was the occasional argument over a game of shove ha'penny on a Saturday night.

A drenching shower had driven us into Mary's — for shelter and beer — on our way back from the Works. Dominating the gloomy bar on that cold May evening was the gamekeeper from Kington Winlow. Marchant he was called. A huge blustering fellow with a nasty temper, a crescent birthmark on his left cheek and an odd twang to his voice that must have come from far west of Devizes. Mr Marchant was the worse for drink.

'No bugger u'll take anything off my patch,' he boasted to some half-demented looking farmhands who seemed to be hanging around on the off-chance of a free round.

A very clever chap he made himself out to be. How he had forty-seven bantam hens under wire and knew — to a bird — how many pheasants he would bring off this year. How there was no poacher known to man who could get the better of him, what with his dog — which was a marvel — trip wires and alarm gun set.

'Impregnable! That's what I be,' Marchant paused dramatically and glared blearily round the dirty, smoke-drenched room. 'Bloody impregnable.'

We went over to Kington Winlow later that night. It was a stiff walk, but the rain had cleared and the downs were silver grey in pale moonlight. We came down from the Ridgeway by a chalk track and turned west along the lower flint road for half a mile or so until we could make out, on our left, the dark outline of the fir plantation that guarded Marchant's rearing field. The plantation was shaped like a horseshoe: a dense fringe of trees and undergrowth enclosing about ten acres of rich sward, with the open end facing away from the downs. Marchant's cottage — an ornate, Swiss-looking affair — was hidden among the trees some fifty yards from the road, at the curved apex of the horseshoe.

Tiger had been to Marchant's place with his father

some years before about some ferrets. According to Tiger, the obvious position for the alarm gun would be at the open end of the plantation – to stop anyone coming in at night from the fields or the valley side of the estate.

It was gone eleven o'clock, I would guess, and you could hear every sound in the night air when we got to Kington Winlow. My boots were soaking and squeaked against the wet grass as we pushed through a hawthorn hedge and crept along in the shadow of the line of dark firs and inky undergrowth that marked Marchant's western frontier.

I was scared all right. But that was why I had started the poaching business in the first place, I suppose – for adventure and danger – the Wiltshire Allan Quartermain. Yet I was unprepared for such jagged feelings of fear. It was not only the thought of Marchant's gun blowing your innards away, but of unseen things – maybe even the Wayland Smith. It was the unfamiliarity of that place at night which was so unnerving: like going into new trenches, in the dark, where a footstep on a duckboard or a drip of water somewhere in front of you can lift the hair on the back of your neck.

At all events, Tiger and I were none too brave on our first visit to Mr Marchant's preserves at Kington Winlow. But we improved. We went back most nights for the best part of a week before we tried for old Marchant's pheasants' eggs.

By that time we had found the alarm gun, screwed to a tree – more-or-less where Tiger had said it would be – and discovered that Marchant kennelled his dog near the cottage at the other end of the clearing, and that he made his last round at nine o'clock as regular as clockwork.

We made sure that Marchant had been in the public at

Liddiard Parva on the night of our final visit, he would sleep more soundly with a bellyful of Mary's beer.

We came off Kington Down at about half-past ten and laid up on the far side of the plantation.

It was a warm night, following a sunny May day with blackbirds singing fit to bust. From our hiding-place behind a clump of cow parsley, I could just make out Marchant's rearing cages like rows of arks in the moonlit clearing.

Everything was as quiet as could be. No sign of Marchant or his dog. There were only occasional rustlings of field mice, the distant screeching of a barn owl. Tiger crept forward to check the trip wire and the gun that Marchant had attached to the trunk of a fir tree. I watched Tiger bend forward, and stand up and then beckon.

That was our first shock: the alarm gun had gone.

The second was worse. It nearly stopped my heart. The snapping of a twig somewhere to our left.

At first, I could make out nothing against the gloom of the fir trees. Then slowly it came into focus, a dark figure standing some thirty yards away. It was unlike anything I could put a name to: slender, with a sort of long cape and something on its head. The figure raised an arm and then beckoned slowly. I remembered Moll Phillips – and her black cat.

'Christ almighty,' Tiger whined at my side. 'What in the hell is it?'

I was too paralysed to answer and just lay there while the figure began to move slowly towards us across the damp grass. As it approached, I made out the pale oval of a face. Then I could see that it was surmounted by a wide hat. Closer still, I saw that it was a black straw one with feathers and two dangling ribbons – Ruth's hat.

Tiger's response was very similar to Jess's when Ruth

pulled the same trick, all those years ago with the little'un, on our way to see the railway engine.

'You stupid bitch,' hissed Tiger under his breath. I could feel his fury in the darkness like a physical force. I was none too pleased myself.

'You'd like as not make a mess of it without I,' Ruth whispered laconically, as cool as a cucumber, as she strolled up to us swishing the wet grass with her high buttoned boots.

My sister had returned from Lambourne the week before. The racehorse trainer, with whom she had been in service had died suddenly and Ruth had had no choice but to come home until something else turned up. She was now twenty-three: a fine young woman, I suppose, with long dark hair – which she coiled on to her head – a turned-up nose, some fancy Lambourne ways and a bicycle. I could smell her scent as she stood close to us. She had had a row with Mother that morning about using the stuff.

'How d'you know we was coming here?' Tiger demanded.

'Not very difficult with you two,' Ruth replied. 'I watched you the other night. Followed on the bike, I did.'

Tiger muttered under his breath. He was shaken, I could tell.

'You can push off back the way you come,' Tiger whispered.

'No I won't. I come for a bit of fun. And there's no telling what sort of mess you two will make of this job.'

'Look, there's a bloody great shotgun, with a trip wire, here somewhere. Old Marchant have shifted it and it'll blow your hat and your drawers off if you sets it off.'

Tiger was beside himself.

'It's *dangerous* here, don't you understand,' he squeaked.

Ruth ignored this.

'What are you going to put they eggs in? That's what you're after isn't it?'

We nodded. There seemed nothing else we could do.

'Right,' whispered my sister, moving purposefully towards the first rearing cage, lifting her long dark skirt as she did so. In a jiffy she tipped the cage over, hauled out a very surprised bantam by the string attached to its leg and stuck its head under her shawl.

'Get hold of they, then,' Ruth hissed, jerking her head, so that her hat wobbled, towards a neat stack of olive-brown eggs.

Quietly and methodically, we moved from cage to cage in the moonlight across Marchant's rearing field. Gradually – and incredibly slowly, it seemed – Tiger and I filled our gunny bags with the warm eggs, laying them carefully between layers of straw, as Ruth lifted the cages and collared the bantams as neatly as an old fox.

Back and forth we laboured in the half-light between the rows of wooden cages, until the gunny bag was heavy on my shoulder.

Then I noticed – on our right – a break in the dark line of firs which, oddly, we had overlooked on our previous sorties. Tiger crept over to it and found a narrow pathway between the trees. He also spotted the alarm gun which Marchant had evidently shifted to guard this entry to his preserves.

Unfortunately, we hadn't reckoned with another of Marchant's tricks: one that any professional would have known.

We walked right into it.

It happened as we were nearing the end of the business

and getting dangerously close to Marchant's cottage. I was holding up a cage, and Ruth was grabbing the bantam's string, when there was an explosion of raucous cackling from one of the remaining cages that made my blood run cold.

Guinea fowls are better than any watchdog and Marchant's set up a clatter that would have awakened the dead. It certainly roused his dog, who joined in the sudden pandemonium.

'Get off back the way we come. And don't drop they eggs,' Ruth shouted. 'Go on! Go on!'

And go we did, as fast as we could, legging it for the open end of Marchant's horseshoe clearing.

The alarm gun went off with a hell of a bang as Tiger and I zig-zagged between the ransacked cages. Looking back, I saw Ruth far behind − pelting along with her skirt held up to her knees with one hand, and her hat clamped on with the other − coming from the direction of the hidden path where, I guessed, she had set off Marchant's gun.

Tiger and I waited for her at the farthest end of the belt of trees and, when she rushed up, took to the open fields at full tilt. We worked our way eastwards, in a wide circle, to the escarpment of the downs and then turned west along the Ridgeway above Kington Winlow to Ashbourne Down. We could still hear the faint commotion of Marchant's dog below us in the valley darkness.

We sang 'Goodbye Dolly I Must Leave You', arm-in-arm on our way back, pushing Ruth's bike until we dropped down into Ashbourne Coombe at well gone midnight.

We were damned lucky to get away scot-free from Kington Winlow that night, with most of Marchant's precious pheasants' eggs. We had so many that Tiger's father couldn't sell them all to the keeper at Hodson and ended up by feeding them to his ferrets. But things might have been very different if it hadn't been for Ruth. By setting off that gun, she must have sent Marchant and his dog in exactly the wrong direction.

Poor old Marchant had no idea who stole his eggs or, to my knowledge, ever boasted again in the public at Liddiard Parva.

He shot himself last year, outside his cottage in the clearing at Kington Winlow.

I've felt guilty about it ever since.

TWELVE

For years I remembered the fair-haired girl who had leaned against the pillar at Liddiard church before Snowball's funeral.

I used to look out for her in the town streets on the way home from the Works, hoping that I would recognise her or that she would come up and speak to me – for I never really saw her face in Liddiard church. In my imagination it had become like Snowball's, with slight freckles, those blue eyes and a mouth that creased in the corners when she smiled.

As things turned out, I was doubly stupid. The girl I had seen in the church was Snowball's cousin, but she was far more like him – as cousins often are – than Mabel, with her short brown hair, dark eyes and straight, but rather bulky, little nose that was less than perfect but thrilled me at first sight.

Mabel just came up and spoke to me one day in the Mechanics' Library – in that gentle, half-amused way of hers.

'You were Snowball's friend, weren't you?' she asked.

I walked back with her that afternoon to the stone cottage near the Works where her mother and father still lived. The next Saturday, I made sure to be in the Mechanics' Library and spotted her again. Mabel told me afterwards that she had done the same thing. She was like that.

So, that rough and tumble in the rickyard at Liddiard Parva all those years ago bore another unexpected fruit.

Mabel was not at all like Snowball, or her sisters – or any woman I had ever known – certainly not like Ruth or Becky. Mabel was merry, sometimes cross, and small and thoroughly modern – like her name – and not the least bit interested in ferreting, or the frame shop, and smelt faintly of talcum, like a clean baby, and walked with her toes turned in ever so slightly, and had pretty ankles. She was interested in ladies' fashions, William Morris and Socialism – she was a paid-up member of the Garment Maker's Union – and was for progress and votes for women. According to Mabel, all we had to do was to sort out a few details for the brotherhood of man to come to pass. It never ceased to amaze me that she could fit an Ashbourne bumpkin into her shining vision. But she did. And that was all that mattered to me in the glorious June of 1914.

We talked of many things, from the sewing of gussets to the sinking of the *Titanic*: I read most of *Bevis* to her sitting on Ashbourne Down with my hand on her skirt and skylarks singing overhead. But there were two things that I avoided. One was her engagement to a wages clerk, Fred Bennett, from the Locomotive Side. He had been killed in a charabanc accident at Dawlish in Trip Week 1912. The other was poaching. Mabel would have been amazed if she had known what I got up to with Tiger and Ruth on dark autumn nights – or any other time of the year, if it comes to that. Looking back, I don't know why I didn't tell her. After all, it was a kind of class warfare, I suppose. But for Mabel the golden age would come by sweet reason, the ballot box and Mr Reuben George: once the privileged classes had seen the error of their ways.

Mabel never ceased to amaze me – like the first time she undid her blouse as we lay on the sward on Ashbourne Down last summer – or the way that she looked at me after she had done it. She never took her eyes from my face. Even in my confusion, and excitement, I sensed that she enjoyed the power that her body gave her over me. Not that I could get her to say outright that she loved me. 'I'm very fond of you dear,' she would say.

Mabel was always slightly elusive. She was like Snowball in that respect. I suppose it was one of the things that made her so irresistible.

I even began to think that things might look up for me. Certainly, I wanted a hell of a lot more from life now that I had Mabel: especially a bicycle. I had longed for one for years. Ever since I started that infernal plodding to work through Liddiard at the age of thirteen. Above all, I wanted a Sunbeam. For months I had lusted after a roadster model – with a natty chain case over its oil bath – in the window of a shop near the Works, at three pounds nineteen shillings and sixpence.

But there was fat chance of my getting one, with what was left of my wages after stoppages and after I had paid my way at home – Mother still made a hell of a row if she didn't get the lion's share – and settled my subs in the Works and bought a few drinks. That is where the poaching money came in. Goodness knows, we made little enough from what Tiger's father said he got for our game – and we had only been at it half a dozen times – but I kept what there was of my portion, in an old tobacco tin beneath a floorboard under my bed. Last July there was one pound seventeen shillings and four pence farthing.

Until Mabel burst into it, my life had been more of an extension of childhood than anything else, with few ambitions more than to sweat it out in the frame shop, sink the odd beer at Mary's on the way back from the Works, or to lark about on Ashbourne Down on fine Sunday afternoons and poach the occasional preserve with Ruth and Tiger and, above all, to stick my head into a book from the Mechanics' Institute at every possible opportunity.

Yet I knew, underneath, that things could not go on like that. I dared hope that, with luck, things might get better for the likes of me and Jess and Tiger and even for Pebbie Titcombe. Mabel had convinced me they would. She was particularly taken with the white man's – and woman's – burden: of bringing justice, and prosperity, to Kaffir and coolie and Brahmin alike. Gradually, and peacefully, the wealth of the nation would pass to the common man, who, being British, would make straight the way through many a far-flung Imperial wilderness. All this she convinced me, between passionate kisses and unbuttoned blouses, would come to pass with the help of the Garment Maker's Union.

'All this' I was indeed prepared to accept, most willingly. But I could see that it was unlikely that I would get a Sunbeam roadster that summer unless I did something pretty decisive.

And that's why I got the others interested in the biggest of our raids – against the Wynyard estate. It was all my idea: I would even tell Mabel about it.

I had listened to some of the men in the public at Liddiard. According to them, the ornamental ponds at the big house were stuffed with trout: huge ones – as big as salmon – just waiting to be lifted from the water.

My plan was to take the nets that we used to drag for partridges. Ruth reckoned that it would need more than just the three of us: two to haul, one to lift the catch and a couple as lookouts, for the ponds were quite near the big house, surrounded by shrubs and hedges enough to hide a regiment of gamekeepers.

So, we recruited Jess and Pebbie: they said that they knew what we had been up to all along. Tiger talked them into joining us. He reckoned that Pebbie was pretty windy at first, but was finally persuaded by the assurance that our first foray would only be for reconnaissance and that he needn't come on the actual day if he didn't want to. Poor old Pebbie. He would have liked a choice like that in Flanders.

We went in at about half-past ten on that warm August night. It was daft really, all of us going in for a quick look round, but Ruth said that we each had to know what we were doing. Jess had difficulty in coming at all: he had to tell his father that it was too hot to sleep and that he needed a walk to cool down. It was easier for Ruth and me. She slept downstairs now on a mattress on the floor; I just jumped out of my upstairs dormer: Tiger's father didn't care what he did.

We cut across the fields to find the ponds, leaving the road from Ashbourne just after the lardy cake woman's house. It was all Wynyard land, but few of the fields seemed to be connected, in the direction that we were heading at least, and there was a good deal of scrambling across ditches and through some very scratchy hedges.

Tiger was leading the way that night, followed by Jess and Pebbie, with Ruth and me bringing up the rear. There were wisps of mist, which, I suppose, was to our advantage provided that we did not lose our way.

The trouble was that none of us had actually seen the ponds or the manor house if it came to that. All we knew were the wrought iron gates and lodge cottage that we first saw on our walk to Acorn Bridge on Chick-Chack Day fourteen years before. The house itself was hidden.

We crossed the last of the farm fields to find a smooth grassy ride, some hundred yards in width, curving gently to the left, with a large statue of a man on horseback standing slap in the middle of it, away to our right.

We padded across the open moonlit grass into the shadows of a belt of tall beeches.

Pebbie stayed there. He was becoming increasingly nervous and said that he would wait for us to return. Poor old Pebbie, I swear that you could *smell* his agitation on the fresh night air.

We crept through the trees to discover, on the other side, more park land sweeping away towards what looked like cedars silhouetted in pale moonlight. The mist had not formed here. I could just make out tiny points of light flickering behind the cedars as we picked our way across open ground: slowly and carefully, pausing every minute or so to look round while a nightjar – goat sucker, as we called them – churred away in the gloom like a little machine.

After what seemed an age, we reached the cover of the cedar trees. There was no sign of any ponds. Ahead was the great house – tall and ornate, with towers and turrets – ablaze with light from dozens of gothic windows. On the terrace were the figures of dark-clad men and women in long ballgowns strolling or leaning against a stone balustrade.

I was mesmerised by Liddiard Hall. No one moved or spoke, we just gawped from the edge of the darkness like the yokels we were.

Then the music started. A real orchestra going at full tilt with a piano and violins and a trumpet.

'It's The Eternal Waltz,' Ruth hissed at my side. 'That's what they're playing. Lovely isn't it.'

One by one and two by two, the guests drifted in through the open french windows until the terrace was empty.

I think we were all drawn by the music and lights. We crept forward, without a word, all thoughts of trout netting forgotten, until, standing in a rose bed, we could see straight into that marvellous room. Everyone was dancing under the brilliant chandelier lights, the gentlemen with their narrow coat-tails flying and the skirts of their bare-shouldered partners swirling across the gleaming floor. One corner of the room was a mass of flowers, and a table was set with glasses and piled with fruit.

'Ain't that wonderful,' whispered Ruth. 'Ain't that just a wonderful thing to see.'

We just stood there among the rose bushes – Tiger, Ruth, Jess and me. Strangely, Tiger seemed almost as affected as Ruth by the spectacle.

After the second waltz, three of the couples strolled back on to the terrace and leaned on the balustrade. Then the men raised their glasses, as though in a toast, turned and strode back through the french windows, pushing through the throng as we stood watching enthralled.

They came round from the right of the big house, riding straight at us on damned great horses across the lawns and gravel paths. There were three of them – in their black tail suits and white ties – lashing away at their mounts. One was the tall, blond-headed man who had drunk the toast on the terrace only minutes before.

'View, haloo – oiks,' he bawled.

'Oiks, oiks – oiks,' the others echoed as we turned tail and made back the way we had come.

They kept coming at us swiping away with the riding crops. One of them got me across the shoulder, and it hurt like hell. They just hunted us like animals that night.

Somehow, I made it to the cedars. Jess was belting along ahead of me and, I seem to remember, Ruth and Tiger were ducking and zig-zagging, on my left. The open stretch to the beech trees was the worst. Three times they rode at me. Each time they slashed out with their riding crops. Once I stumbled and fell and felt a hoof brush against my hair.

I picked myself up and, somehow, got to the beeches, while the horsemen harried Jess as he sprinted, twisting and turning, towards the dark trees.

I hid in the undergrowth until the hallooing and a faint drumming of hooves died away to the left. There was no sign of Pebbie Titcombe. Where Ruth and Tiger had gone I had not the remotest idea; Jess must have been close at hand, but I couldn't see or hear him. The only thing for me was to push on across the grassy ride, through the last belt of trees and out into the open fields. Now everything was silent, except for eerie screeches of barn owls and the churring of the goat sucker still going away where I had last heard him. I headed to my right, the way we had come, hoping to reach the road to Ashbourne.

I pushed through a gap in a hawthorn hedge. There was a sudden break in the clouds and the landscape was flooded with moonlight. In the middle of the field were the three dark horsemen. I pulled back into the hedge, which was hollow, as they often are in the Vale of the White Horse, and trotted along to the far end. There was no way through from there, but running along at my feet I could see clear water, sparkling in the moonlight, flowing away to the right.

I splashed along that stream like a lunatic. But even in my panic, I knew where I was and what was behind the hedge on my left. In a jiffy, I was out on the road and in through the wicket gate which I had pushed open so hesitantly all those years before.

All was silent in the lardy cake woman's garden: she had passed on twelve months before, but I still thought of it as hers. I slumped down beside a row of scarlet runners, winded and drenched to my waist, cursing poor old Richard Jefferies to bloody hell – on that night of August 3rd, 1914.

PART THREE

Ypres

THIRTEEN

It's odd that I can recall, in such detail, so many things about Ashbourne. Even the walk to Acorn Bridge. That was fifteen years ago, but I can remember the pressure of the gravel through the thin soles of my boots as we scrunched our way up to the church where we saw the old woman's corpse, even the sound of bees and the calling of jackdaws in the elms, and the smell of water plants, that first astonishing glimpse of a locomotive at full lick, as we stood gawping by the Wilts and Berks Canal. I suppose it's because of the shaking up I've had and the endless hours in hospital wards with little else to think about.

Yet nothing could have been further from my mind that morning, six weeks ago, as we moved up from our reserve Company position. For two days Fritz had been pounding away at Ypres. Its distant white towers still gleamed, ghostlike across the flat Belgian countryside, amid smudges of black smoke and occasional flashes of flame, as huge German shells crashed into the stricken town. To our left, the ground rose gently for a couple of miles to a low range of scraggy hills topped by a broken windmill.

With the coming of April, the weather had improved

and was now springlike. Only days before, the fields had been tended — as neat and green as the Vale of the White Horse — right up to the support lines. Now the whole flat landscape was churned and pitted by shell-holes, with blackbirds chittering from shattered tree-stumps, as we marched in file, by sections — in platoons and companies — to the singing of skylarks, the jingling of mess-tins and accoutrements against our webbing equipment, and the monotonous hissing and exploding of German heavy shells away to our right: swish — boom . . . swish — boom. . . . A Boche Albatros circled overhead. I could tell, from the jaunty angle of his rifle, that Jess was excited. Tiger had gone ahead with the new subaltern. He did a peculiar thing before he left: surrep-titiously fishing out a strip of faded green silk from his pack and shoving it in his tunic pocket. He didn't know I was watching, but I recognised it all right. It was the gold embroidered band that Tiger pinched from the Bible at Liddiard Church, although it looked a good deal the worse for wear.

The German bombardment of our position started as soon as we began to file behind the camouflage screens into the reserve trenches. The Huns must have been waiting for us or, perhaps, tried to catch us in the open. Some French 75mm field batteries opened up with rapid fire, but failed to stem the tornado of exploding shells and flying soil.

'Steady lads — keep your mouths open and your eyes shut,' the sergeant bawled, between explosions, as we crouched like babies on the fire step — hands clapped over our ears — the ground shaking like an earthquake and sandbags slipping from the parapet.

After an eternity, the maelstrom gave way to a baleful silence. There was no birdsong now — nor the sound of any living thing. One by one we slowly stood up on the muddy duckboards, still dazed and shaking but dusting down our uniforms and picking up our rifles.

I pulled out Ruth's letter from my pocket, tore it open, still half mazed, and squatted down on the fire step to read it.

Then came that dreadful German afterthought – the gigantic explosion at the very edge of the next section of trench.

I felt my feet lift beneath me and the trench wall seemed to move upwards. There was a tremendous blast of air which tore the cap from my head and pressed against my chest and spine. The sun was dimmed by the rain of soil.

I awoke to find myself lying along the parapet, looking up at the pale blue sky. There was no pain. I couldn't move my legs and something seemed to have happened to my back. I must have passed out after that, although I remember being bumped about on a stretcher as darkness fell. I can recall nothing more until I came to, stuck against the canvas wall in a corner of the field dressing station. Tiger was with me, I seem to remember, and then went away. The lamplight hurt my eyes. They fixed my legs as best they could, I couldn't feel them at all for a while, and said they would get me out of the line soon.

All I could do was to lie there and wait – and think.

The last batch of walking wounded left before I did. One of them was in the Wiltshires, a Highworth chap from O Shop with his head bandaged and an arm in a sling. He sat with me after they finished with my legs. A proper chatterbox he was about the Works: said he could see that the War was coming, though it was still a hell of a shock when the factory hooter sounded all those times last August. He had thought it would never stop and just stood there with his mates in the middle of the O Shop, until the noise finally stopped and then he went back to the job he had started before the War.

Everyone seems to remember what they were doing when war broke out. It was warming up to another real scorcher in the frame shed that morning when the hooter sounded. I was setting up a new job with Fred Stratton, I remember, and worrying about that business with Tiger, Ruth and Jess at Liddiard Park the night before.

The Highworth bloke said he had seen us Ashbourne lads at the recruiting meeting in the Mechanics' Institute. Everybody was there: we had followed the band of the 7th Wiltshires for the best part of that Saturday afternoon. The hall at the Institute was packed. Tiger, Jess, Pebbie and me jammed in at the front of the balcony to hear the big pots going on about our duty and dear old England and being worthy sons of our forefathers. It was as hot as hell. Bummer Pinnell was there with his mates and a whole crowd from G shop and Bodger and Stiffy, from Ashbourne, with a sprinkling of Wootton Bassett lads from the Carriage Side. We queued after the speeches to sign on. Jess signed first, scrawling in his signature with a flourish.

We were grand fellows again that night – like we had been on Chick-Chack Day all those years before – striding back along the road through Liddiard Parva shouting and singing the old Boer War songs and kicking at the thistles and wayside flowers in the half light. Although, in truth, we were pretty long in the tooth compared with the seventeen-year-olds who had signed on that night.

There was a red glow behind Ashbourne Church. Closer to, we could see flames consuming the last of the Church Farm rickyard. Granny Bowles was watching from her cottage gate. She was convinced the Germans had started the blaze.

'Don't you worry, Missus,' Pebbie called to her. 'Us'll

see off they Germans for you when us gets across to France.'

Poor old Pebbie. It was surprising that he lasted so long out here. Everyone knew that he was windy – *and* about his craze for animals. The only time I knew him risk his skin was when he stretched out over the parapet to grab a bull frog.

Even the N.C.O.s did their best to keep him out of the way if there was any trouble. I can't remember Pebbie ever being sent under the wire, like that Wootton Bassett lad who Mr Fletcher always took with him if he could. The two of them would be out almost every night, if the weather was right, until poor little Fletcher got it. His family were solicitors at Trowbridge, Jess said.

I suppose that's why they used Pebbie as a runner when a Jerry barrage cut the telephone wire. It would at least get him out of the way for a while. When he didn't return, I thought he was napoo. But it turned out Pebbie had just kept on walking down one of those straight, poplar-lined roads, like he had wanted to along Ashbourne Lane when we had that spot of trouble outside the pub at Liddiard on our way to Acorn Bridge.

Pebbie was trying to slip round a police post at a level crossing when they caught him. He got Field Punishment – not lashed to a limber or anything like that – but they chased him from hell to breakfast-time, including burying a dead horse. It rained continuously and Pebbie blubbed.

No sooner had the Company moved back to a support position, than C. S. M. Young sent Pebbie forward, with a lance jack from Wroughton and a detail of other defaulters, to collect the poor devils who had been brought in during the night. Some of them were from our Company and had been dead as doornails for days.

They dug the grave – a big square job with plenty of

room for everyone – in mushy dead ground behind our position and had started lining up the occupants, ready for the chaplain, when Jerry shells burst overhead. They all jumped into the pit, crouching alongside the corpses, until the shrapnel subsided and then crawled out – all except Pebbie who was lying face down with blood splattered over his back.

They left him and just covered him over when the Padre arrived: it seemed the right thing to do, the lance jack said.

Not everything out there was bad. Even Pebbie laughed sometimes.

We were so close to the Germans once you could hear them talking and larking about in the trenches. Often there would be calls for 'Müller' and then laughter and shouts of 'Bravo, Müller' and the like.

Next day, the shout went up from our lads: 'We wants Müller – we wants Müller'. Pebbie was yelling with the best of them. We kept it up until a helmet appeared abruptly above the parapet of the German trench, then a head and the shoulders and, more slowly, the torso of a small bespectacled man, lifted by hidden hands. Not a shot was fired by the Wiltshires and great was the cheering from our platoon as Private Müller bowed gravely to us before being lowered from sight.

We also heard the Germans on Christmas Eve, playing mouth organs and melodeons and singing as though they had not a care in the world. We sang 'Christians Awake', and such like, and 'The Vly Be On the Turmit'. All night we kept it up, one against the other. Yet we were waiting for them that cold Christmas dawn standing to, as usual, on the fire step with our rifles ready. As the mist rose, we saw them sitting on the tops of their trenches and waving to us. We waved back. No one fired. Then, one-by-one, we clambered out of our muddy, stinking prison (Jess was one of the first) and edged our way through the wire while the officers argued between themselves about what should be done.

One of the Germans – a tall fair-headed fellow, with a broad, slab face – spoke good English. They were Saxons, he said, which I thought funny because that was what our King Alfred was supposed to have been when he kicked hell out of the Danes near Uffingdon Camp. There were some dead Warwicks lying on the frozen ground and the Jerries helped us to bury them.

Some of the Saxons were country lads. They hated Prussians, they told us, and were homesick for Saxony – wherever that was – where the land was good, with rolling hills and a wide sky.

Which were exactly my feelings for Ashbourne and the Wiltshire Downs, although it had taken Richard Jefferies to show me that.

I wonder what Jefferies would have made of the trenches? Bevis would be too old for this lot, forty-five by now, I should think. The trouble with Mr Jefferies was that, for him, our sort were just part of the landscape, his beautiful Wiltshire landscape. The *bastard*! I remember how he was going on in one of his books about farm kids, locked out of their cottages – like we were, and lurking around the rickyard on winter afternoons, snivelling with the cold. According to Mr Jefferies, they were tough little beggars, much healthier than town children with their boots and warm clothes.

And there was bloody Bevis bossing Loo, the half starved farm labourer's daughter, who had waded across to New Formosa, their secret island, to steal food. Bevis got all indignant, and then patronising, when Loo told them her father drank, and sent her home with a tin of preserved pheasant. Not cake, mind you, like Marie Antoinette, but tinned bloody pheasant.

It might have happened to Ruth if that lot at Liddiard Hall had found her as a child scrounging at the kitchen door instead of gawping through the ballroom window as a grown woman.

Funny I didn't think of it before.

I suppose I have always been secretly ashamed of that business at Liddiard, on the night before the War began. Something had happened to Ruth then. She had had the stuffing knocked out of her, yet I couldn't discover *how* or *why*. She said her skirt was torn while pushing through hedges, there were scratches on her neck and her right arm was bruised. The riders never struck her or rode her down. She and Tiger had escaped quite easily she said, though they took so long getting back that night. They said they'd been half way to Highworth to work their way round to Ashbourne.

I suppose it could have been the shock and humiliation that upset Ruth — the hunters hunted, like animals, in the summer darkness. That was what stuck in my gullet. Ruth's as well, I reckon, for Mother always said that the two of us were more alike than any of the other kids.

Tiger was beside himself after the Liddiard disaster. He swore that if it was the last thing he did, he would get back at those toffs, hamstring their horses, set fire to the Wynyard stables, borrow a gun and blow their bloody heads off.

I must say, Tiger worried me. He had been alone with Ruth for a couple of hours that night. It would have worried me a hell of a lot more if I'd known how he would carry on outside the *estaminet* at Poperinghe after we had been there for delousing. According to Jess,

Tiger suddenly made a grab for the mademoiselle at turning-out time and tore her dress. The others pushed him out of sight of the Military Police patrol in the dark street. He would have got Field Punishment if he had been copped and that would have been the end of Tiger, for I am sure that he would never have knuckled under.

He has always been a mystery. It was the last thing I expected that morning, as we moved up the line near Ypres, when Tiger volunteered to go ahead with the new subaltern. None of us had ever seen the man before. It was not a thing I would want to do − crawling about on your belly in broad daylight under the wire, or whatever else, a perfect target for a Jerry sniper. Tiger had said that he was from Ogbourne when the officer asked where he came from, which seemed odd to us, and he was on his feet and off like a shot when beckoned. He was lucky to have gone as things turned out. At least he escaped that last bloody great shell.

Tiger re-appeared in the dressing station while I was still lying there in the dim lamplight. I opened my eyes to find him crouched down beside me. He tried to get me to drink some brandy from his water bottle. He said that Jess was in a bad way in the trench when he had left him. He had been hurt even before the gas came in a dense, yellow-grey cloud that drifted over from the Hun trenches towards the Algerian lines. The Poperinghe Road was bedlam, Tiger said, but he had managed to keep ahead of the gas. Jess must have pegged out as it caught the edge of our positions.

Tiger wanted to know if I had had Ruth's letter. I nodded. It had been in my hand when the shell exploded. He asked me if I had recognised the new officer. I shook my head.

'He was one of them three that came after us on horseback at Liddiard, last summer,' Tiger whispered. 'I thought I recognised the bugger because I got a good look at him when your big sister and me got behind a gorse bush and they stopped to look round – right in front of us – before they chased after you and Jess.'

There was a distant rattle of machine-gun fire. Tiger crouched down instinctively and spoke straight into my ear.

'That's why I went with him just now. But I needn't have bothered – I don't think it was him anyway – and a Jerry sniper got him before I did.'

Tiger peered down at me: he looked as if he thought I was done for. His eyes were darker in the soft lamplight than I remembered them. Then he fished about in his tunic pocket and pulled out a narrow strip of faded green silk, embroidered in gold, and draped it carefully across my chest.

'I looked after your Ruth that night, in a manner of speaking. That's what the letter's about. How'd you like to be an uncle?'

There seemed nothing to say. I couldn't answer anyway.

He smiled, his face strangely softened.

With that, Tiger slipped away.

I never saw him again. They took me out of the line soon after Tiger had left me lying there on the stretcher in the lamplight. They told me I had shrapnel wounds in my left lower leg and foot. Later, they discovered that blood had leaked into my spinal cord from the blast of the explosion. It was Blighty for me after that. First, the Bristol Royal Infirmary, with views of roof tops and factory chimneys, and now this rambling great place, near Totnes, with turrets and twiddly bits all over it just like Liddiard Hall, only three times the size. You can see glimpses of the River Dart between wooded slopes.

The nurses wheel us out on to the terrace on sunny afternoons when the officers are taken in for their tea. Then I get to thinking of Tiger and Pebbie and Jess.

At night, sometimes, I wake up in the ward in a sweat as the sapper snores in the next bed. I can hear the owls hunting outside, along the lush Devon hedges, like I used to at Ashbourne, and a fox barking across the coombe. Last night, I kept thinking of those screams in the darkness behind the German lines. It had rained continuously and our trench was a quagmire with the duck boards sinking into the mud. Twice we had heard her, faint but clear in the night air. The second scream had gone on for a minute or more, like a wailing from eternity. Then there was silence. No one spoke. We just stood there on the fire step, staring into the damp February gloom.

The Saxons had gone out of the line sometime before. They had shouted over to us before they left, that they were being relieved by Prussians.

'Give us time to get out, Tommies,' they called. 'Then shoot the bastards.'

There were no more shouts from the Jerry trenches, no Private Müller, only the whiplash crack of rifle fire, the occasional machine-gun rattle and those screams in the dark.

I shrank within myself at the memory. I imagined Ruth, lying in the mud with her skirt pulled up to her navel, and Mabel, her blouse falling around her waist, a Prussian bayonet at her breast.

I still think of Mabel, most of the day, especially when one of the officers sets his gramophone going.

One tune he plays over and over again. It always makes me think of her.

> And when I told them how beautiful you are,
> They didn't believe me . . .

Mabel used to make me sing it to her, but I would always start laughing before I was half-way. Then, pretending to be cross, she would fling herself at me and we would end up wrestling on the downland turf with the whole of the Vale of the White Horse at our feet and the skylarks singing overhead.

Mabel had seen the show from which the song came. *The Girl from Utah* it was called. She had gone to London on a garment factory excursion to a matinée at the Gaiety Theatre. In the summer of 1913, I suppose it was. She had wanted me to go with her last year to see *The Belle of New York*, but I didn't want to be the only man with a parcel of women.

I met her at the railway station afterwards. It was late, gone nine o'clock, when her train came in. She was excited; wearing her dark blue dress with the white sailor collar, her eyes were shining. Her hair was fluffed up more than I had ever seen it before. Mabel kissed me that night outside the railway station in front of her friends, who went 'Oooh' at the outrageousness of it. It was only a peck on the lips, but I knew then that she was not ashamed of me.

There has been no sign of Mabel since I've been back from Flanders, not even a postcard. Ruth brought her baby yesterday and stayed the night somewhere in Totnes. He's tiny, with a squashed-up nose, dark eyes and looks about a hundred years old. I am not sure that Ruth should have travelled so soon. We sat on the terrace together this afternoon, looking across the valley, while Nurse Drew made a fuss of the babe.

It seems Mother has been putting it around the village that Ruth and Tiger had got married on the quiet, and at the last minute, before we all went off to the War. Now that Tiger's gone as well, I suppose her story will be safe, although I doubt that it will fool anyone in Ashbourne.

I can still see Ruth walking away from me down the curving gravel drive, between the rhododendrons, in the late afternoon sunshine. Nurse Drew had found an old wickerwork perambulator for her from somewhere and Ruth has her valise across it. She stopped, to wave, holding on to her hat. Then she made that funny little punching movement of hers, with her right arm, as she did when she jabbed me in the belly on the walk to Acorn Bridge.

They will be haymaking in Ashbourne when she gets back.